A Journey To True Love

A novella by

Alisha Coleman

Copyright © 2015 Holloman Publishing

ISBN: 978-0-9897274-6-4

ISBN: 0989727467

Introduction

In life we all want or desire true love. As little girls we dream of our knight in shining armor or the magic of our first kiss. Boys want to be superheroes. The journey we take to find this love is different for everyone. Our past experiences, life choices, and view of what love is determines this path. The young superhero becomes the man that wants to save the woman from hurt and pain of the world. The journey we take can be clouded by pressure from our friends and family or the negative thoughts of society. Having a true love is only determined by the two people in the relationship. Your definition or reality of love determines your success in finding and embracing truelove.

This story follows six college friends as they journey through life in search of a true love. Mike fears loving the woman of his dreams, causing him to lash out and settle for what he believes is Miss. Right. Sydney met her first love in high school and settled for his friendship, but never revealed her feelings to him. Toni and Luke we in love and wanted to spend their lives together, but the lack of communication hindered their relationship. Staci married Doug after college and their love has blossomed, but will a secret tear that love apart? These friends are in search for success, happiness, and love. Their search for success, happiness, and love takes different paths throughout this story.

Enjoy this story while reflecting on your own journey as you embrace your true love.

Chapters

Chapter 1

"It's time Syd." Mike said as he and his best friend sat in the living room that evening.

"Time for what Mike," Sydney asked looking puzzled.

Mike sighed as he gazed into the darkness of the room while the music played in the background he leaned deeper into the sofa. "It's time for me to ask Kelly to marry me, but I'm still not sure if she's ready or not." Sydney stood up from her comfortable spot on the floor and turned off the music. "Why do you feel like that?" she asked as she walked over to Mike. "Didn't you say she was pushing you to get married a few weeks ago?" Sydney sat down on the sofa next to Mike. "She was," Mike said, sitting up, "but I was waiting for that big promotion and it hasn't come through yet. I can't marry her without providing her a certain lifestyle." Sydney rolled her eyes at Mike because she knew that was a dumb reason but she also understood her friend and his beliefs. "Mike, women don't care about your money when they get engaged." Sydney patted Mike on his leg to show comfort before continuing. "She doesn't care about a position, she cares about is you."

"Syd you know all women what a man that can support her.

"Mike you can and will."

"But Syd you don't understand..."

"I understand you're making unnecessary issues because you make enough to give to her now." Mike stood up and walked towards Sydney. "I understand that, but I wanted to keep her in a lifestyle she's grown accustomed to living." Sydney stood up with frustration. "She doesn't have a job, so what lifestyle is she accustomed to living? I guess the gold digger wins again". Mike became angry and shouted, "It's better to be a gold digger than a femme fatale!" Sydney rolled her eyes, saying, "That was low Mike but your little Miss. Goodie Two Shoes has several flaws." Mike shouted, "Sydney you haven't dated a man for over two weeks and Kelli is perfect!" Sydney stormed back into the room. "Well Mike, you said that about Victoria, Mason, and that back to nature or natural girl!" Mike walked closer to Sydney and looked her eye to eye. "Her name was Amaryllis, and she was awesome."

"Oh yes and they all cheated on you in some form or fashion." Sydney snarled. Mike walked away from Sydney as he

pondered the truth. "Kelli is different,"
Mike quickly turned towards Sydney, "She
still pure and waiting to get married, unlike
you." Sydney burst into laughter. "Ha, I'm
sure she's been on her back and knees too
more than once." Mike grew concerned and
tried to be more considerate. "Syd you're
just lashing out because I'm in a beautiful
relationship and yes, I will move out soon,
but we will always be friends." Sydney
walked off towards her room as she
continued to laugh at Mike. Mike laughed
as he recalled the silly disagreement they
had as he walked to his room to prepare
for bed.

Mike awake refreshed and humming to
the music he turned on every morning so
he could dress; while dancing and
reminisce about his day. Within ten minutes

a song came on that reminded him of how sweet and innocent Kelli is, so he called her. He dashes to the night stand and called the woman he loved. Kelli's phone rang. She searched for it with one hand and her eyes still closed, but after five rings a groggy Kelli found her phone, "Hello."

"Good morning to you baby."

"Mike, why are you calling me so early?" she moaned as she glanced around the room, but her search came up empty. "I called to check on you, so how are you doing this morning?" Kelli moaned and stretched as she glanced around the room again before responding. "I'm okay, but why are you calling me so early?" Mike felt uneasy, so he made up something. "I remembered that we are having lunch with your parents today, so I wanted to check in with you on what I should wear this time?"

Kelli sighed with annoyance. "Mike, wear the suit we bought last weekend... oh, and I put all the accessories in the bag." Mike sighed with relief because she did not seem upset. "That is why I love you." Kelli smirked and whispered, "I know and making you a success is why I'm in your life. And Mike, don't call me this early again."

"I'm sorr..." Kelli hung up before Mike could finish his response.

Sydney yelled from the other room, "Mike, are we still meeting for drinks later, I want you to meet Steven." Mike yelled back, as he continued to get dressed, "I finally get to meet this dude, but Syd we are having drinks here tonight." Sydney walked towards Mike's ensuring she heard him correctly because she set up that date two weeks earlier. Sydney was dating Steven exclusively yet and wanted to leave their options open just in case her friends didn't approve. "Mike when did you plan drinks here?" Sydney stuck her head in the door. "I wanted you to meet him since you both have something in common. He's the Chief Financial Officer of a major company and you're putting in for a promotion." Mike popped out of the bathroom while tightening his tie and pushed the bedroom door closed to get his jacket. "Syd, I sent group texts out last night remember?" "No." She said thinking about their fight last night. "But any way, what do you want to do about meeting him tonight?" Mike looked puzzled and uneasy because it was about Kelli tonight and he did want her to get upset if Sydney's news keeps her out of the spotlight. "Syd we don't have a lot in common. Maybe you and a job, but you can invite him as long as you remember it's about Kelli tonight." Sydney sighed as she tried to hide her true feelings about his stupid statement. "But Mike, you two both love golf, tennis, westerns, and working out." Mike did not want Sydney to invite Steven, so he tried to discourage her. "Sydney, are you sure that bringing him tonight would be a good idea after what happened last year."

Sydney chuckled, "Bill, I almost forgot, but he was a good liar."

Mike smirked, "Sydney really?" The bed room door flew open and the deep baritone of a familiar voice followed. "It's about time you guys have taken you relationship to another level."

Mike was startled. "Hey man, I didn't hear you knock."

Sydney was noticeably, "Luke, please stop getting up his hopes."

"I didn't Mike because I used my key." Luke looked puzzled.

"Wait, where did you get a key?" Sydney asked looking at Mike.

Mike eyes pleaded with Sydney. "I gave it to him when we went on that trip a few months ago, but you were not supposed to find out." He gave Luke a hateful look and snatched the key out of his hand. Luke tried to snatch his hand back, but Mike got the key before he reacted. Luke smiled, "Sorry Mike. Come on Syd, I need that key for when I move in here with you." Sydney walked out shaking her head. "Man, leave her alone she's upset about me getting engaged to Kelli and she doesn't have a man yet."

"Wait, you're marrying Kelli?"

"Of course, are you so surprised?"

"Well the main reason is, you're madly in love with Syd since high school."

"Man, that was a long time ago and we were kids."

"That's because you never tried again and pawned her off on other guys," Luke chuckled, "or were scared because you've been doing it since high school."

"Well in high school they called us the princess and the frog, so to protect her I decided we should end the relationship."

"That was your junior year, so what happened after the prom and college?"

"She was dating the quarterback, but took me to the prom because he was sick. I dated Monica Stanfield after prom night." Luke laughed. "Oh yeah the chick that used you and broke your heart because she was just using you to make her boyfriend in college jealous."

"Man forget you." Mike said as he walked towards Sydney's office. "Syd I'm gone and don't forget we are having drinks tonight at seven."

"Bye Mike and Luke have a great day."

"See you tonight Syd."

Sydney walked into the kitchen to get a cup of tea before starting her day. After she powered up her computer and read a few emails she took a break and called her girls to find out if they were coming over tonight. Toni's phone rang twice before she picked it up, "Girl I have something to tell you."

"Can it wait I want to call Staci too."

"Yes Sydney, because you're going to tell her anyway," Toni laughed. Sydney called Staci on the other line and as soon as the phone rang, she merged Toni back into the call. "I'M EVERY WOMAN IT'S ALL ABOUT MEEE..."

"What are you crying about Toni," Sydney asked.

"Now the question should be who, is she crying about?" Staci asked sarcastically.

"That's right she had a date with Mister last night," Sydney exclaimed.

"Yes I did, so stop hating you lonely heifers."

"Wait Toni we both have men," Staci exclaimed.

"But, Miss goodie Two Shoes isn't putting out and you're married so we know you're not getting any." Toni laughed.

"Just because I'm picky, doesn't mean I'm a Goodie Two Shoes Toni." Sydney exclaimed.

"No, it means you need to stop waiting for

Mike." Staci said as if she were telling a secret.

Toni laughs. "Yea before you become a bitter old maid because as long as Mike has money Kelli isn't going anywhere."

"I'm not waiting for Mike and I met a great guy thanks to Staci," Sydney touted.

"You'll meet him tonight for Mike's big surprise."

"I told you Steven was different."

"Wait, who is Steven and why didn't I meet him first," Toni asked bewildered.

Staci exclaimed, "Toni you are not his type and Doug said we should set him up with Syd."

"So now your husband gets to decide who I meet." Toni said with a sigh.

"Now Toni, you're not ready to settle down, so don't even go there." Sydney said as she shook her head.

"Sydney I told Mister last night I wanted to stop playing and move towards something serious."

"Who is Mister," Staci asked.

"That guy Toni met a few months ago and now she's in love."

Toni and love don't even fit together," Staci laughed.

"I say that he's married because I haven't met him and she only talks to him at certain times."

"Well Toni if he's married he's not trying to settle down with you. Get down maybe, but settle down, that's a big fat no." Staci exclaimed.

"If he had a woman he's leaving her for me anyway."

"Didn't Henry tell you that last year after you found out he was married," Sydney asked.

Staci gasped, "Honey you should be tired of all these run down men that have a woman at home and do a background check before you get all caught up."

"She does a background check on their wallet and bank account because that's all she cares about" Sydney laughed.

"I do care about them Syd and Staci I always check for a ring, but if a man is taken why would he ask me out?" Sydney and Staci burst into laughter.

"So on a lighter note, are you guys coming over tonight."

"Yes, but is everything okay?" Staci questioned.

"I'm sure everything is fine Mike just wants to show off for that thang he's dating."

"Toni that's not nice." Staci exclaimed.

"Yes it was because I could've called her

what she is such as a slut, trick, a hoe not whore, stank bi..."

"Toni stop, you might be right, but you're wrong for saying it behind his back."

Sydney said as if she were chastising Toni.

"I agree with Syd, Toni."

"You would Staci. But Syd she's not right for your man."

"My man when did Mike become my man?"

"Since you were in high school."

"High school, we dated for like two weeks and decided to be friends."

"No honey," Staci said calmly. "He decided to become friends not you."

"Whatever that was in high school and we are grown now."

"Girl you can't break the spell of your first love."

"Is that why you and Luke are always fighting Toni?" Sydney asked.

"Come on ladies be civil."

Toni grunted, "You make me sick Staci with your polite behind always trying to do the right thing."

Thanks Staci. Love you ladies, but I have to get this work done." The three ladies hung up after saying their salutations hoping to see each other later that night.

A few hours later as Sydney was finishing up her paperwork when her phone vibrated across her desk. "Hello."

"Hi beautiful," his deep soothing voice caressed her ear as he responded.

"Steven, how are you today?" She said trying not to giggle like a school girl.

"I'm doing great," he smiled. "I got your text this morning, but I knew how my day would be and I didn't want to call you until things slowed down."

"So what you're saying is, you had a hot date last night and overslept so you couldn't call." She laughed.

"Didn't that sound better than telling you I was with my ex last night."

"Really, so what does that mean for us?"

"She's an ex for a reason but unlike you I like sex, so until we are serious I will continue to have sex."

"Why did you guys break-up?"

"She was a gold digging daddy's girl, so she wanted me to take care of her and I need a woman that understands responsibility." Steven paused. "I need a woman that knows how to do more than shop and sleep all day while I work or refuse to cook because she can't mess up her nails." Steven sounded upset.

"Forgive me for bringing it up."

"Baby it's not you. I was in love and

wanted to marry a trophy, but since I've met you I'm having second thoughts."

"Now that's the sooth talking man I love talking to on the phone." Sydney giggled. "So, are you going to be here tonight?"

"I wouldn't miss it for anything. I can't wait to meet your friends."

"Well, they are not like Staci and Doug so prepare yourself."

"See you around 7:30 because I have to finish this report and I have my last meeting around 5:30." Steven said glancing at his watch. "That's fine, I'll see you then." Sydney smiled as she dwelled on how a future would be with him. "Bye beautiful." Steven hung up and Sydney lay back in her chair with a huge sigh.

"Well son you will get a big promotion soon and you are doing good for yourself, so what is your next step?" Mr. Mathews questioned a nervous Mike while the women cleared the table. "That's why I wanted to talk to you in private, Sir."

"We can talk on the balcony in my office." Mike jumped up and followed the older well reserved gentleman to his office. Mr. Mathews turned towards Mike, "Do you smoke cigars," as he cut the end of one of his finest Cubans and handed to Mike.

"Well, son what do you want to ask me?" Mr. Mathews bellowed as they walked onto the balcony. "I would like to marry your daughter." Mike's words rushed out so fast he didn't remember saying them. "Calm down young man I won't hurt you for doing the right thing; which is rare these days." He patted Mike on the back. "Why would you want to marry my daughter?"

"She beautiful, I love her, and she's smart."

"Do you respect her?"

"Yes sir." Mike quickly exclaimed.

"Have you bought a new house yet?"

"No sir, I wanted Kelli to pick out the house she wanted after we said I Do."

"Are you living with another woman?"

"No, I mean we have been best friends since high school, so after college, we bought a house together because we couldn't afford to live alone."

"Have you been intimate with this girl?"

"No sir we are just friends and we have never dated."

"You can marry my daughter but you must find a house before the engagement party that's suitable for my daughter."

"Thank you sir," Mike said as his voice quivered.

"Don't thank me yet, because if my daughter has any issues with the house or that girl, the engagement is off and you can't marry my little girl."

"Yes sir and I will honor your request."
Mike was concerned about the whole
situation because his friends did not like
Kelli. If he moved out now Sydney would
be hit hard financially because she started
her own business a few. "I know son." Mr.
Mathews said as they walked into the great
room with the women.

Mr. Mathews looked at Mike. "Kelli,
Mike has something to say to you." Mike
got on one knee in front of Kelli, "Kelli I've
waited all my life to find a woman like you.
I'm willing to spend the rest of my life
fulfilling your every need." Tears caressed
Kelli's eyes and rolled down her cheeks.
"Kellie Mathews will you spend the rest of
your life with me?"

"Yes Mike, I will." Kelli spun around in the

middle of the floor. "Well done son." Mr. Mathews said as he watched his daughter dance with joy. "I can't wait to show off my ring to your friends tonight, will Sydney be there?"

"Yes, but she already knows."

"You told her before you asked me?"

"Yes, but she's my best friend."

"I thought Luke was."

"They both are." Mr. Mathews cleared his throat as a reminder to Mike about their discussion. "But you're my best friend now, so can you forgive me?"

"I will this time." Kelli quickly kissed Mike and ran towards her room. After she disappeared up the stair case Mike hugged her mother and shook Mr. Mathew's hand. Mr. Mathews said, "Don't forget what we discussed son," as he patted Mike on the back.

Mike went back to the office and was distraught about telling Sydney he was moving out because of Kelli soon than they had planned

Chapter 2

Mike and Sydney were setting up for the gathering. As Sydney brought in a tray of fruit and cheese Mike turned down the music. "Sydney I need to talk to you about something very important after everyone leaves."
"What is it Mike?"
"I said I'll talk to you about it later."
"Hello, my name is Sydney and you act like you just met me."
"No Syd, it's just I have so much going on I don't want to forget."
"Is everything okay?"
"Yes, but I need to take care of something's after tonight."
"Okay." Mike cut on the music and Sydney went into the kitchen to get the wine. The front door flew open and a deep bass tone saying, "Party over here," was the only sound heard. "Where are all the single ladies?" Luke bellowed. "Luke you're louder than the music and this is not a party." Mike frowned, "Where's Christine?"

Sydney walked back into the room with the wine and laughed at Luke trying to ignore Mike. "Luke I said, where is Christine?"

"Man, she's at home with her mouth stuck out because I won't give her a ring."

"Well, I don't blame her," Sydney said, "so when are you going to make an honest woman out of her and stop playing house with her?"

"She doesn't work, has her own credit cards, and her own car; therefore, why buy a cow when you can overdose on all that free milk she's giving?" Luke laughed uncontrollably. Mike tried to hold in his laughter because he agreed with Luke.

"You have a serious problem Mr. Dark Ages because you're acting like a caveman." Toni shouted.

"Wait Toni you can't talk where's Mister?" Sydney asked.

"He said he had to work late."

"Toni when are you going to wake-up and smell the coffee, dude has a woman." Luke exclaimed. "Shut up Luke."

"Look you two we are here to celebrate not fight."

"He started it."

"Shut up it's not my fault you're so easy, I mean easily misled." Luke walked into the kitchen behind Sydney to help. Toni sat on the sofa after pouring herself a drink. Mike was looking through his phone to find the right song for his announcement. Luke grabbed Sydney by the arm and looked around before he whispered, "What is Mike about to do?" Sydney looked around the room and whispered, "Ask him." Luke turned up his mouth and picked up the ice bucket. "I know he wants to marry that chick and I will put her on blast."

"What are you talking about?"

"She's not right for Mike and she's a liar."

"I have no proof and this chick has Mike's nose open we need proof."

"She's having sex with his boss so he can get promoted."

"Mike said his father knows him and put in a good word."

"I have to catch her before my friend is trapped by that succubus."

"May he'll wake up soon."

"After she's sucked him dry," Luke snarled

as he snatched up the ice bucket he filled with ice and put it on the cart with the decanters.

Twenty minutes after seven Kelli arrived mouth first, "I'm here so you can celebrate me, my ring, and our new house." Everyone looked at each other while Mike ran into the kitchen. "What are you talking about now, crazy woman?"
"Mike and I are engaged and will buy a new house this month."
"Really, wow I'm so happy for you." Toni said sarcastically we turning up her nose.
"Yes really you bitter little... let me go find my man." Kelli stormed out of the room to find Mike. Staci walked into the house.
"Looks like I got here just in time, so we can change the subject." Staci walked over to Sydney and whispered, "Steven is outside parking his car." Sydney smiled and ran to the door. "Who is Steven?" Luke demanded.
"He's her new man." Staci blurted full of excitement.
"When did you get a man Syd," Luke asked

looking concerned.

"From what I heard she let someone else pick him out for her." Toni shouted.

"Who picked what for whom?" Kelli asked as she walked into the room with Mike.

"Sydney's new boyfriend," Staci said full of excitement.

"Is he real or a figment of her imagination because she's jealous of me and Mike?" Kelli snorted. Mike quickly grabbed Kelli and led her to the sofa. "But Mike tonight is about me not Sydney and her desperate cries for attention."

"I'm sorry baby but you'll have your own engagement party soon."

"You are sorry and if things don't change there will be no need for a party or this ring." Kelli folded her arms in a huff and turned her back to Mike.

When the doorbell rang Toni pushed Sydney out of the way, so she could open the door. "Well hello sir, I'm Toni."

"Toni, get out of the way and let the man in the house." Luke yelled. Steven walked towards the living room with Sydney.

"Forgive me Steven but these are my friends, everyone this is Steven."

Kelli jumped up, "That's who?"

"Baby calm down. That's just Syd friend." Mike said as he reached for Kelli's hand.

"Fine as wine, sexy, and yes any day or whenever you want it Steven, I'm Toni," she said as she shook his hand.

"Toni, calm your hot behind down and let the man breathe." Staci laughed. Luke walked over to Steven. "Nice to meet you Steven, I'm Luke." Mike walked over after Luke shook his hand. "Hey man it's nice to meet you." Mike pulled Kelli closer. "I'm Mike and this is my fiancée Kelli."

"Fiancée huh, well Kelli it's nice to meet you." Steven said with a polite smile.

"Yeah whatever I need a drink Mike." Kelli staggered back towards the sofa. "What's wrong with that chick now?"

"Who cares Toni, oh Mike?" Luke laughed. "I guess all that fineness is causing her to have hot flashes." Toni laughed.

Kelli jumped up and ran over to Toni. Kelli screamed, "Does your loose ghetto a... I mean behind ever tire of listening to the crap that flows from your disease infested lips?" Mike ran over and pulled Kelli out of the room. Luke laughed, "Now that was the pot calling the kettle black." Luke turned towards Steven and said, "Welcome to our dysfunctional friendship." Steven laughed, "Well that's women and the life we live with some of them." Luke patted Steven on the back. "Man. I like you already; yea, we will be good friends."

Toni pursed her lips, "You would like a man against women."

"Wait Toni, I'm not against women. I do not like the ones that resemble the pot and love to call out other women out."

"Heck, I like him too Luke." Toni laughed. Staci put her hands on her hips. "All of you are out of order."

"Stop being our mommy Staci," Toni stated.

"Steven would you like a drink to go with your entertainment?" Sydney asked. "Yes Sweetie, Do you have Hennessey?"

"Yes."

"I'll have that with a shot of cola and two ice cubes."

"Staci I'm glad you didn't set me up with him because he's too picky."

"Don't worry I would not have given you a second look anyway." Everyone laughed. Mike walked into the room as they were laughing. "What's so funny?"

"Steven called Toni out on her stuff."

"Whatever quick draw."

"I got your quick draw." Luke said.

"Yeah I remember you couldn't hold it then." Toni said as everyone laughed.

"Well you never complained in college, so I guess the quickness satisfied you." "All right you two, we can at least pretend in front of company." Sydney coyly said. "Syd if you don't stop acting I will turn my jokes on you."

"Luke stop! Sydney is right; you don't want to give Steven a bad impression of you." Kelli walked into the room and Mike quickly jumped up to give her his seat. "Staci's right, so let's focus on me and the house Mike will buy us before our engagement party...and you are not invited." Kelli sneered.

"New house, Syd you didn't tell me that

Mike was buying a new house." Toni said.
"There seems to be a lot of not telling everything going on around here." Steven stated.
"What do you mean by that," Mike asked, concerned about his statement.
"Nothing man, so how long have the two of you been dating?"
"About a year and a half."
"That's a long time, and you just got engaged?"
"Well I had to get my finances together."
"Oh you mean make more money." Steven said with a smile.

"Okay it's time to play games everyone." Staci shouted
"There goes the white woman again, so what do you want to play Jenga or Yahtzee?" Staci was about to respond when Luke cut her off. "Look Staci we want to dance, so turn the music up Mike."
"Make it slow because I want to dance with my baby." Steven pulled Sydney closer.
"Look out there now." Sydney said.
"Come on Luke and dance with the white

woman."

"I want both of the single ladies," Luke shouted.

"Well I want to dance with my man and he just text me, so I'm out." Toni ran out the door after gathering her things. "Bye tramp." Luke said as Toni was closing the door. "You're just made because you can't have all this."

"No I'm lucky because that means I'm disease free."

"I hate you."

"Good." Luke kept dancing with Staci. "Bye Toni, I'll call you tomorrow."

"Syd walk me to my car." Toni could wait for Sydney to close the door. "Did you see the way Kelli acted when she saw Steven?"

"Toni doesn't start."

"Sydney I know that look. Something or was going on with her and Steven."

"It doesn't matter because it was at least two years ago."

"Okay but when the crap hits the fan remember this night and what I said."

"Good night Toni, go enjoy your man."

"Well watch your man around her." Sydney

hugged Toni and walked back into the house.

"Okay, it's time to play games" Staci squealed.
"Let's play a game before this woman drives me crazy." Luke sighed.
"We can play charades." Steven suggested.
"That's cool, Mike set up the game." Sydney said as she cleared the table.
"Man, I should've brought my girl."
"I told you to bring her." Mike said while setting up the board.
"Man I wasn't going to bring her around that bitter Toni."
"You didn't feel that way in college." Staci blurted.
"That's right you did date in college." Mike laughed.
"Next subject."
"Oh yeah, you broke off the engagement after you caught with her Charles." Sydney laughed. "It was Charles, and he was fine as wine and every girl wanted him, but Toni was the only one that saw his jump shot up close and personal."

"Why y'all gotta bring up the past, let's just play this stupid game."

"So Luke you had a woman you were engaged to cheat on you too." Steven said. Kelli blurted, "Well she was probably unsure of her feelings and gave up to make sure they were real."

"Sounds like you've been there, but you know we are talking about Toni?"

"I have a close friend going through that now, so I know her pain." Steven sat up and asked, "So did your friend screw the man she loved one day and get engaged to another man the next day?" Luke shouted interrupting the conversation. "What the hell, this ain't Oprah."

"Sydney seconds Luke's response. "Luke is right, so are we going to play this game or what?"

"Come over here with me and Sydney Kelli because we are about to whip some man butt."

"I agree Staci. Come on Kelli we are going to tear them up."

It's time to regain our championship belt, right Luke," Mike shouted.

"That's what I'm talking about we are going to tear those behinds up. Come over here with Mike and me Steven."
"Bring it on cause we ain't ever scared." The ladies shouted.

They played for a couple of hours before Staci started getting sleepy. "Well I think it's time for me to get home to my hubby."
"Sydney, I don't think I can drive after hanging with Luke."
"I should've warned you about Luke and his heavy hand."
"That's because Luke always spends the night Steven." Mike said as he laughed.
"Can I stay over tonight Sydney," Steven asked.
"No you can't. You can catch a cab or something, but I'm not staying in a house full of strangers." Kelli shouted. Luke responded, "Man you can stay. We don't let folk drive drunk."
"Well I don't like it and since this is almost my house too, I think he should leave." Kelli said as she waved her arms all

around. "You can sleep in my room so Kelli will feel comfortable."

"The hell he will Miss. Sydney. I refuse to sleep in a house full of ill will."

"I almost called you something; go sit your raggedy behind down somewhere. Mike, get your girl," Luke bellowed.

"Kelli baby calm down. Syd's a big girl, but she's not like you so we can't expect her to control herself."

"Mike I know she's your friend, but what is that supposed to mean?"

"Kelli is waiting until she gets married before she indulges in fleshly satisfaction."

"Is that what she told you?"

"Man not you too."

"Man I was just shocked, but that's your girl and your beliefs so my opinion does not matter."

"Yes you're right your opinion doesn't matter because we are waiting until we get married unlike Syd."

"That's cool. Kelli it's good to hear you are saving yourself for marriage." Kelli stormed off towards Mike's room. Luke laughed uncontrollably. Mike realized he was not going to like Steven. Sydney and Steven cleaned up the living room.

After Sydney and Steven finished the dishes they went to her room, so they could retire for the evening. Sydney gave Steven some sweats and a shirt that Luke gave her earlier. Sydney took a shower after Steven. When she got out of the shower, she dressed in sweats and jumped onto the bed. "Steven, do you know Kelli?"
"Why did you ask me that?"
"Well you're the first person besides Luke to rattle her cage and make her feel uncomfortable."
"I just have that effect on women." He kissed Sydney on the back of her neck.
"Really," Sydney said, snatching away.
"So how long have you and Mike been kicking it?"
"What do you mean?"
"Well the brother isn't blind."
"No it's not like that. We've been friends since high school and after college, we bought this house because it was a good investment."

"So you never gave him any?"

"I told you I've never had sex."

"So why did he say all of that stuff about you?"

"Because I've never dated so many men he thinks I can't keep one because I'm too easy."

"Sound like he's jealous to me."

"Mike, never looked at me like that even in high school."

"So tell me how long has he been with the stuck up chick?"

"Almost two years.?"

"That long huh."

"So how long have you been single?"

"It's been so long I've lost count

"What about you?"

"I told you it's been six months, but she calls me every day."

"Have you given up on her yet?"

"Yes last night after I slipped up and had sex with her."

"How long were you together?"

"It would've been three years yesterday."

"Why did you break-up?"

"She didn't want to sign a pre-nup, so she

left and came back less than a week later."

"Why was it an issue?"

"She didn't want to work, but wanted to be taken care of, because she's a spoil little brat."

"I know that's Kelli, she's a realtor but she's never sold a house. I guess that's why you make her so uncomfortable because you can smell the fake on her."

"That's not all I smell." Steven kissed Sydney on the forehead and turned over to go to sleep.

Kelli and Mike were having a heated discussion in the room. "Kelli is there something you need to tell me?"

"No Mike."

"Then why are you so upset about Sydney and Steven?"

"It not right. He seems like a great man and he deserves better than your slutty roommate." She hissed.

"Wait only I can say that about Syd. You don't have a right to judge her."

"Why, all you do is complain about her going out with these different men, so you know what she is."

"She's a lovely woman that any man would be lucky to have."

"I was just trying to help out."

"Kelli she's never had sex in the house or had a man stay over here, so I think it's safe."

"But they could be doing it right now. I'm going over there to put an end to that right now."

"Get back in this bed, heck you act like he's your man."

"Go to hell Michael." Kelli screamed. She stumped towards the bed and threw a pillow at Mike. Mike sat down in the chair holding the pillow she threw.

Chapter 3

Sydney was up before anyone else as usual and started breakfast. Once the smell hit the air Luke came down the hallway. "Hey what are you doing up so early cooking. You're already taking care of your man."

"Luke I'm cooking for everyone, not just Steven and you know I do this almost every day."

"That means he didn't hit it last night." Luke laughed.

"Who didn't hit what?" Mike asked as he adjusted his robe.

"Steven didn't get any last night."

"Man she's never given it up at home anyway; I guess she's scared I'll hear her." Mike and Luke laughed as they gave each other high fives. "Man she's not giving it up anyway."

"Excuse me but she's right here and what I give is my business."

"Yeah that's right my woman is a real lady." Steven kissed Sydney on the neck.

"Can we eat yet?"

"Yes Mike but where is Kelli."

"She's still asleep." Mike and Steven said in unison

"Y'all did that in surround sound, do it again." Luke laughed. Mike gave Steven a funny look. "Luke stop being silly." Sydney said as she hit him with a dish towel.

"Sorry but I know her type."

"And what is that?"

Luke responded before Steven could.

"Stuck up because she's rich, spoil, and...Oh you weren't talking to me."

"No, I wasn't."

"Well she seems a little mean, spoil, and selfish."

"I think you need to focus on your own girl and her actions."

"I do, so I know I have a gem and not some counterfeit crap." Luke was laughing so hard at Steven's response he could barely catch his breath. "Now that's what I'm talking about, preach brother. You know the truth and you just met that..."

"Luke you need to tone down that loud ghetto talking because you woke me up from my beauty sleep. Good morning Stev...I mean Michael."

"What did you just say?" Luke inquired.

Sydney quickly interrupted, "Nothing, now let's eat."

"Oh my, Sydney you're a good domestic." Kelli chirped.

"She's the kind of woman every man desires." Steven announced.

"Well every man wants an easy woman." Kelli barked.

"I'm sure her innocence's trumps yours," Steven boldly announced.

"That's what I'm talking about. Gold digger 0 and good man touchdown," Luke said, as he stood up to make a field goaled. "Forget you Luke."

"I wish you would forget all of us." Luke remarked. Mike turned to face Steven, "Look man I don't know you, but I refuse to allow you to disrespect my future wife or my house."

Luke became annoyed with Mike. "Man you've let Kelli disrespect Syd in her house since day one, so how is this any different? This dude just met her and can see what it took months for me to see or for Syd to accept." Mike stood up in a huff. "Come on baby let's go on the deck and finish our breakfast."

"I hope you used protection last night." Kelli snarled at Steven. "Well unlike you her legs don't spread like butter on hot toast." Luke laughed at Stevens remarks.

"Steven stop Mike is my best friend, and she's going to be his wife, so we need to get along."

"Forgive me, but that woman rubs me the wrong way."

"Man don't feel bad, she has that effect on everyone."

"Luke you need to stop because she had your tongue hanging out at one time too."

"That's because she was fine and before she opened her mouth letting me know she was the bride of Satan." Luke laughed.

"I think that describes her best."

"I know her type and they all fit the same mold."

"Sir that is another thing I can agree with you on that, but I must excuse myself and take a nap before I go home to this fight.

Syd thanks for breakfast, it was delicious.
Steven it was great meeting you and I hope
you stick around because I need some help
to keep Hagatha in her place."
"It was a pleasure man because Sydney
deserves more respect that she or Mike
give her."
"Thank you, guys."

Sydney started washing the pots while
Steven cleared the table and loaded the
dishwasher. "I think we will make a great
team Sydney."
"Really?"
"Yes really." Steven walked up behind
Sydney and kissed her on the neck. Sydney
responded by turning towards Steven
giving him their first kiss. "Sydney I need
to tell you something because I think we
are starting to get a little more serious."
"What is it Steve?" she asked nervously.
"I didn't know until last night, but..."
Kelli walked into the kitchen mouth first
cutting Steven off. "Steven what Are you
doing?" Kelli ran out of the kitchen and
bumped into Mike without stopping. "What

did you do to her now?" Mike yelled.
"We were just kissing Mike." Sydney
responded as if she was pleading for him to
forgive her. "Sydney you know how she
feels about that kind of stuff. Look Syd I
love her therefore I must protect her, so
you made this easy. I need you to buy my
half of the house from me so I can move
out."
"Mike you know your timing is bad for me
right now."
"That's not my issue Kelli is, so figure it
out or we can sell the house."
"Don't worry Sydney I'll help you."
"There you go, your knight in shining
armor." Mike walked out the room in
anger. Steven rubbed the small of Sydney's
back to show her support. "What in the
world is going on in here, I thought I was at
home."
"Kelli saw us kissing and got upset, so
Mike told Sydney he's moving out and she
needs to buy his half of the house now."
"He knows you just bought that property
for your new business and poured all of
your savings into your dream."

"Don't worry baby I'll help you in any way I can."

"Steven I just met you a couple of months ago and we are still dating other people, so I can't let you do that."

"Why the hell not?" Luke asked in amazement.

"I'm a business man first so I can accept that. Let's do this, sell me a percentage of your business for Mikes half of the house."

"But I don't know you like that."

"You know Staci and Doug right?"

"Yes, but..."

"You can trust them right?"

"Yes."

"I have done business with Doug, so that's one reference and since I do not mix business with pleasure I will get my lawyer to draw up a contract, but it will be in your favor."

Luke jumped in, "Syd I have a friend that's a corporate lawyer and he owes me a favor, so I'll get him to look over the contract for you."

"Baby girl, I'm going to take care of you."

"Syd I think this dude is a keeper. But I

need to talk to Mike because that girl has him on some crazy crap. I can't believe he would do this to you."

"Love will make a man do some crazy things Luke." Steven said.

"That's why I keep those four letter words out of my vocabulary."

"Was that before or after Toni." Steven laughed.

"Man I was just starting to like you and then you sucker punch me." Luke and Steven walked out of the kitchen, while Sydney finished putting everything in order.

Mike walked into the kitchen looking like a lost puppy. "Syd, I'm sorry, but her dad wants me to move out of the house with you before our engagement party or the wedding is off. That's what I was going to tell you last night.

"That's cool but I don't accept your apology because you've allowed that woman to disrespect me on so many levels." Sydney leaned against the door jamb. "Mike my question for you is, when are you moving out?"

"That's cold Syd, but I'll get the process started next week." Sydney walked out of the kitchen when Mike sat down. Luke patted Sydney on the shoulder as she passed by him. When Luke entered the kitchen, he sat at the table with Mike.

"Now Mike you know that was foul." "Luke don't start."

"Man Sydney has been your best friend for years, so why would you do this to her?"

"This coming from a man that constantly cheats on his woman that's perfect and treats him like a king."

"See that's where you are wrong, I've never cheated on Christine while we were together, but we are talking about you and Sydney, the woman that's been there for you through thick and thin."

"Just because she helped me out once doesn't mean I owe her anything."

"Yes you do because as her friend you at least owe her respect."

"Man I respect her."

"No you don't because Sydney hasn't had sex with anyone but you're always calling her easy."

"well she's not a virgin."

"Mike, Toni would always talk about her saving herself for that one man and until I met Steven I didn't think she ever had sex."

"That's because she dates a man for two weeks and he dumps he, so what is that?"

"what makes you think they dump her?"

"Because Todd went out with her and he said he hit it the first night, but she got too clingy and he dropped her. Now if she let Todd hit it and got that way anybody can get it."

" Man I can't even believe you listed to that dude because that is not what happened."

"How do you know."

"How do you know Syd doesn't talk to you and Todd hates your very existence."

"Toni told me."

"Toni told you and you're not cheating, but you believed that gossiping home wrecker?"

"We've been visiting her grandmother every other weekend since college."

"Oh yeah, I forgot about that."

"Toni said Todd tried to take Syd to a secluded location so he could have sex with her, so she jumped out the car and ran. Toni picked her up, and she spent the night with Toni. Mike Syd's been hooked on some dude since college and was waiting on him, but I guess since she's with Steven things have changed."

"Who is this man?"

"Toni didn't say and I didn't ask."

"Does Christiane know you still visit Toni's grandmother?"

"Does Kelli know you're in love with Syd."

"Man. I'm not in love with her anymore."

"Well by you actions I can't tell."

"What?"

"Mike you never defend Kelli or let her talk to Syd like that without saying something,. But last night you did. The only difference was Steven."

"That's not proof, man I need to go check on Kelli, so I'll leave you alone with your ridiculous thoughts."

"The truth hurts doesn't it, man be true to

your feelings." Luke laughed as Mike walked out of the kitchen.

"Steven are you going to hang out with me for a while or did Kelli scare you off?"
"That girl could never do that, but I have a 9 o'clock tee and I cannot miss it."
"Are you going to stand me up for golf if we start dating?"
"No, but this is business so I have to go." Steven paused as if he wanted to say more.
"Sydney there are some things I want to tell you, but because I have to leave, it would not be fair to you to start a conversation I can't finish."
"I like the way you think, but I do have one question."
"What is it?" Steven had one hand on the door.
"Should we start moving towards dating exclusively?"
"I asked you that before I met your friends, so the ball is in your court."
"Okay we will talk later, come give me a kiss." Sydney ran over and kissed Steven.
"I'll call you later." All Sydney could do

was smile. Steven ran down the stairs and out the front door. Sydney was floating and thought this couldn't be real. She floated downstairs to lock the door. Sydney watched Steven as he drove off before going upstairs.

Mike and Kelli were having a heated conversation about the events that happened that morning. Kelli was so upset she couldn't stop crying. Mike was scared he might lose Kelli so he decided to look at houses online to calm her down. "Hey babe, let's look at houses online so I can get an Idea of what you want." Kelli jumped and dried her eyes. "What's your price limit?"
"I want to start off at 300,000 but not over 500,000."
"Why so low?"
"Baby I want to get the promotion before I buy a house bigger than that."
"That doesn't make any sense because you have credit."
"Kelli, I work in finance, so I know not to spend above my means."

"Daddy said you were going to get the job."

"Kelli I still don't know what my salary will be because those jobs have a weird pay scale."

"I'm calling daddy right now, so pull up this house." Kelli handed Mike a card with a name and number. She walked out of the room to call her father. Mike pulled up the site and typed in the ID number for the house. He almost fell off the bed when he saw the price of the house. Kelli ran into the room. "Mike when you go in on Monday you will have your position." Mike looked puzzled. "I understand that, but what about my salary?"

"I forgot to ask, but how much do you want to make?" Mike was dumfounded at the question. He knew the position's top paid man received 900,000 in pay and another 125,000 in bonuses. Mike was in a place that he didn't think he was ready for. "I'm not use to having these kind of connection."

"Well if you're going to marry me, you better get used to it."

"I will just let me bask in this blessing."
"One thing you never do, is tell someone
thank you when they help you out. Please
don't talk to my daddy about this because
he's doing me a favor not you." Mike felt a
little funny about her statement because of
the things Luke said about her. "What's
wrong Mike?"
"Nothing baby, I was just in awe of the
things you said."
"Well Mike, that's what happens when
you're with a woman like me."
"I see." Mike was beginning to rethink this
whole marriage thing. Kelli saw that Mike
was getting scared and knew she had to do
something to reel him back in. "Mike go
take a hot shower, so you can refresh your
mind." Mike got up and walked into the
bathroom. Mike tried to give himself a pep
talk before he stepped into the shower.
Kelli searched through Mike's phone to see
who was pressuring him to leave her alone.
She checked his emails, but found nothing
there either. Kelli knew she had to get
Mike back under her spell or he would
leave her. "Mike?" Mike didn't hear her

over the noise of the shower. Kelli jumped up and ran into the bathroom. She took off her clothes and opened the shower door. "Kelli what are you doing!" Mike exclaimed. "I just wanted to caress you Mike."

"I need you to get out because···"

Kelli grabbed his manhood. She slowly caressed it until she could embrace the fullness of his desire. Mike could barely catch his breath, "I really needed that release. Thank you baby," Mike said. Kelli gently kissed Mike on his chin and walked out as smoothly as she walked in. Mike finished his shower as if nothing happened, but all of his thoughts were of pleasing Kelli. Mike walked into the bedroom after he finished taking a shower, "Kelli, you're a beautiful woman and I'm so lucky to have you." Kelli was still wrapped in the towel as she rose from the bed. "Mike you are going to be my husband, so I have to be aware of the pressure you're under." Mike smiled because it was a confirmation of her love and his friends were wrong about her. "I am going to tell my father to throw the engagement party and we will buy a house after we get married."

"Thank you Kelli."

"You are so welcome, baby."

"Trying to get a house before the engagement was a lot to swallow, since I have no idea what my salary will be."

"On Monday you will and then we can plan the wedding."

"What about the engagement party?"

"My dad has hired someone for that, but I am planning our wedding."

"Is your dad going to agree to all of that?"

"I'm my daddy's little girl, so he will do whatever I want him to do."

"I guess you have that effect on all the men that love you." Mike kissed Kelli on the forehead. "Oh Mike you are just right for me." Mike blushed. "I'm going to take a shower and then we can go out for a late lunch."

"That will be fine." Mike lay back on the bed and thought about how good Kelli made him feel.

Sydney was sorting out her clothes when she was startled by her phone. "Spill it, did you sleep with Steven?"

"Yes I did and we slept through the night."

"Okay Staci she's trying to be funny."

"I told you she didn't have sex Toni."

"Syd if you don't have sex soon your vagina is going to close up and you'll never be able to have sex." Sydney and Staci laughed. "Toni is that how you first convinced you to have sex?"

"No but that's what I told him, so he could save me."

"Her first was Luke so we know that's a lie." Staci stated.

"I know Staci and all this sleeping around crap is a bunch of talk."

"How do you know Sydney?"

"Staci, she's never brought any of these men around and she calls all of them Mister."

"I call them Mister because I don't want to say their real name by mistake and you have met them."

"Toni I've only met the ones you call by their real name and there was only one married man."

"Well even one is bad Sydney."

"She didn't know he was married Staci for three months and then she broke it off."

"Syd you don't have to tell all my business."

"Well Toni you need to stop walking around here like you're a home wrecker."

"Sydney is right Toni."

"How did the subject flip we called to see what was up with Syd and Steven."

"Your adventures were more interesting than mine."

"Her life has always been more interesting than ours Sydney." Toni cleared her throat. "Like I said did you have sex with Steven last night Syd?"

"No I did not have sex with Steven last night Toni."

"Well what happened because Luke told me it go heated over there."

"Luke told you," Sydney pursed her lips as she paused. "When did you talk to Luke?"

"You know we still love to gossip and since Christine isn't speaking to him, he called me to find out what's up with you and

Steven."

"Why does he want to know about me and Steven."

"Well from what he said Kelli has the hots for Steven and can't control herself around him."

"You and Luke were messy in college and you're messy now." Staci exclaimed.

'Staci we are not messy we just like to laugh at y'all on a journey to find true love folk." Toni laughed. "Luke and I are happy single, but since we've known Syd and Mike they have been searching for love everywhere, except in front of them."

"Toni I am not on a journey to find true love because I have it with you guys, my best friends."

"That's sweet, but lets get back to Steven." Staci chimed in, "Yea I'm with Toni."

"We decided to become exclusive."

"All right now." Staci cheered.

"I'm so excited!" Toni sang full of joy.

"Wait ladies, there are some things we need to discuss before we seal the deal."

"You mean have sex."

"No Toni, before we make our relationship official." Sydney looked at her phone.

"Ladies I have to do Steven is on the other line." Sydney clicked over, "Hi Steven.

"Hey Syd," he paused and took a deep breath.

"What's wrong?"

"I have to leave town in a few hours, so we won't be able to talk until I get back from this business trip."

"That's fine."

"No it's not. I almost forgot about it but my assistant called me to let me know he checked me in."

"So, what time does you flight leave?"

"In less than three hours and I'm still at the golf course."

"Are you going to make it in time?"

"Yes my assistant is going to my house to pick up my things...he should be here by now."

"Well call me when yon land."

"I will, talk to you soon. Steven quickly hung up and Sydney rolled over on the bed disappointed.

Chapter 4

Mike and Sydney were discussing the issues they were having since he started dating Kelli and why had not invited to the engagement party. Mike was drinking a lot more than usual. Kelli walked into the house screaming for Mike. "Hey babe, I'm glad you're here. Will you get me a cool drink because I'm exhausted?" Mike jumped up, "Okay baby." He stumbled over to kiss her but she pulled out her cell phone to avoid his advances. Mike quickly turned his attention to the kitchen, so he could fulfill Kelli's request. "Hello Kelli."

"Hi Sydney. Oh darn!"

"What's wrong Kelli?"

"My phone just died, can I use yours?" Sydney reluctantly handed Kelli her phone.

"Thanks sweetie, but this is a private call so I'll be right back."

"Where's Kelli?"

"She asked to use my phone so she could go make a private call."

"Why is she using your phone?"

"She said her phone was dead."

"What's that noise."

"You phone is ringing Mike, man are you that drunk?"

"That's not my phone." Kelli bounced back into the room all bubbly. "I thought you said your phone was dead."

"It is!"

"Then why is it vibrating?"

"That's strange, I thought it was dead."

"Whatever." Sydney snatched her phone out of Kellie's hand and walked out of the room. Kelli sat down next to Mike, "So did you finish signing all the thank you cards?"

"Kelli I didn't know any of those people at our engagement party."

"That doesn't matter and you should be happy because I convinced daddy to go through with the party even though you haven't moved out."

"But Kelli that was your idea and now there is tension between me and my friends."

"How much have you had to drink?" Kelli smirked.

"Maybe two or three."

"Okay, well you better kiss and make up because the wedding is soon and I don't want any ghetto drama from your friends."

"My friends are not ghetto."

"If you say so, well I need your card to pick up some things tomorrow." Mike pulled out his wallet. "Here and don't go crazy this time."

"I'm worth it." Kelli smiled and ran out the door.

Mike poured himself another drink before turning on some music. Sydney walked into the living room to check on Mike after she ate dinner. "Mike are you okay?"

"Yes as long as she gets what she wants."

"Mike all women get like that when planning their wedding."

"I bet you wouldn't."

"I might not ever get there at this rate."

"What about Steven?"

"He's great but I think he's going to tell me he's still hung up on his ex, I'm just a rebound." Sydney picked up the empty bottle Mike had on the floor next to him.

"Syd you could never be a rebound."

"I thought so too until now." Mike pulled Sydney into his lap. "I love you Syd."

"I know Mike now let me go."

"I've While they were talking always loved you Syd."

"Mike you're drunk, now let me go." Mike pulled Sydney even closer and kissed her. "I wish I was marrying you." Sydney snatched away from Mike looking confused and ran upstairs.

When Sydney got to her room she locked the door, but was panting heavily. Her phone rung and startled her, "Hello."

"Girl what's wrong with you."

"Nothing Toni I just ran upstairs."

"If you say so. Are we still going to lunch next week?"

"Yes and yes my treat."

"And I get to pick."

"What's his name?"

"William and he is single girl," Toni shouted.

"Well I'm happy for you," Sydney sighed.

"So what happened to Mister, he went back

to his wife?"

"No he was cheating on both of us with a younger man."

"Wait he was bisexual?"

"No he had a son that neither one of us knew about and I don't share my man's money."

"You are crazy."

"Yes I am."

"So what's up with your boy Mike?"

"We talked about the issues we've been having since Miss. Thang came into the picture."

"No I mean when are you and Mike going to lay your cards on the table?"

"At the same time you and Luke get back together."

"I read you diary in college."

"I can't believe you Toni."

"Well believe it, but your little secret is going to die with me."

"Why would you do that?"

"I thought you wanted Luke, but you were really sweet and innocent."

"Okay, nobody wants Luke but you and Christine. And you cheated on Luke, so why would you think that?"

"I wasn't cheating, but your girl Staci was like me now."

"Doug was her first."

"No it was Cornell and that's why Luke thought I cheated."

"But I thought you did."

"No I was keeping Staci's secret."

"What?"

"Remember that little trip we took and you got mad because we didn't tell you?"

"Yeah it was after finals and you had Luke distract me."

"Yeah."

"So what happened?"

"I can't tell you."

"Well Rita Jones told Luke that you cheated on him."

"Why didn't you tell me?"

"Because you would've beat the crap out of her and got kicked out of college."

"You better be glad Mister is on the other line." Toni hung up to answer her phone.

Toni was so busy watching the couple in another booth, she didn't hear Sydney.

"Toni who are you watching?"

"Isn't that Kelli over there looking real friendly with that man?"

"Where?"

"On the left behind that tree on the left."

"Yes, but I can't see who she's with."

"Well I'm going over there to confront her."

"No don't do that because we need proof or Mike won't believe us and she'll twist the story in her favor."

"Dang she's leaving, I'm going over there." Toni jumped up and ran towards the door. "Hello Kelli."

"Excuse me, but do I know you."

"Don't play with me chick; I'm Toni Mike's friend."

"Oh the ghetto mistress."

"Well today you seem to be the ghetto whore, so who was that man you were with?"

"Lady I don't know you so please get out of my face." Kelli pushed pass Toni. "I'm telling Mike!" Kelli smirks as she walked out the door. "Toni what are you doing?"

"I'm trying to...isn't that Steven?"

"Where?"

"At the bar."

"Yes." Sydney walked over to the bar, "Hey Steven." Steven was startled, "Sydney what are you doing here?"

"I'm having lunch with Toni."

"How long have you been here?"

"I just got here a few minutes ago. Toni saw Kelli with another man, so she chased her to the door when she got up to leave."

"Who was she with."

"We couldn't see him behind that tree." Sydney looked at Steven's hand. "What's wrong Sydney you look as if you've seen a ghost?"

"I'm okay I just need to get something to eat." Sydney rushed off before Steven could say goodbye. "What's wrong with you?"

"Why are people asking me that?"

"Because you look like you've seen a ghost."

"Nothing is wrong, did you order?"

"Yes, I ordered steak for me and got you crow."

"That's fine just get mine to go."

"Syd did you hear me?"

"Yes I need a drink."

"I guess you realized it was Steven?"

"What?"

"I told you months ago that Steven and Kelli had something going on."

"We're still not serious yet, so it doesn't matter."

"Kelli is about to marry your best friend and you look as if you've seen a ghost, so it matters."

"Why did you do this to me Toni?'

"Somebody had to save Mike, but I didn't know Steven would be here."

"I don't care because he won't believe me."

"Well do to him what I did to you because he needs to know."

"I can't do that to Mike."

"Why not!"

"Because he will hate me forever and we just started talking again. Mike will not be able to handle this."

"Yes he can."

"Then you do it because it would be obvious if I brought him here."

"Why?"

"Toni we drove forty-five minutes away to get to a place that's twenty minutes from our house."

"Well we have to do something."

'Yea, but this is going to kill him."

"Well it's better late than never."

"Toni they were just having breakfast, so that doesn't mean anything."

"Did you not see how they were interacting?"

"Well she was the only one moving he seemed to be pushing her away. I need more proof." Sydney stood up to leave.

"Okay, but don't forget Staci's dinner party next weekend." "I'll be there, but I'm not sure if Steven can face me again." Toni stood up and hugged Sydney. "I'm sorry Sid and maybe it was innocent." Luke walked over to Toni after Sydney left the restaurant. "What did she say?"

"We need more proof. Did you know about Steven?"

"No I was just as shocked as Sydney, but if we need more proof I'll get it,"

"If you knew about this why didn't you tell Mike?"

"Mike is way too sensitive about that girl."
"This is just like college, you had Sydney
tell him about that girl too."
"Look men don't have those sensitive
moments like females so I can't tell him."
"But Luke, you play the role of a female
dog in heat so well."
"Bye Toni." Luke stood to leave. "Call me
later because I think I have an idea." Luke
flirted with the hostess as he walked out.

That Saturday Mike surprised Sydney
with a picnic. When they were in college,
they would hang out in the park after finals
all the time. Mike and Sydney walked along
the lake throwing bread to the ducks. "It's
been a long time since we've done this."
"Yes it has." Sydney was looking somber.
"What's wrong with you Sydney?"
"Nothing, I'm just thinking about the last
time we were here."
"Yeah, that was crazy." Mike kissed her
hand. Sydney snatched her hand back,
"Mike what you are doing!"
"Sorry I just got caught up in the moment
because I realized how awesome you are

as a friend."

Sydney turned up her nose, "Really?"

"Why are you looking at me like that?"

"Mike what if I told you not to marry Kelli?"

"Wait where did that come from."

"You kissed me and said you love me. You said you wanted to marry me instead of Kelli."

"I just had cold feet."

"Do you remember what you said?"

"No I can't remember what I did in a drunken stupor, but I do love you as a friend."

"Well I guess that's that."

"What is it that you're not telling me?"

"I'm just scared that you're making a mistake and she's going to hurt you."

"Syd I know you're concerned, but I'm a big boy, so does this have anything to do with Steven?"

"What, Mike we are not that serious."

"Well he was the first dude that stayed after you gave him some, by the way have you been tested or did you used protection?"

"I needed the same protection that you
needed with Kelli."

"Well Kelli and I never had sex."

"You mean you never penetrated her.
Steven and I haven't done anything, so you
need to get tested before you marry her?"

"Syd are trying to say Kelli is cheating on
me?"

"Yes!"

"Do you have any proof."

"She was the woman I saw with Steven
that day."

"You really need to stop hanging with that
psycho Toni."

"What are you talking about?"

"She called Luke and told him the same
thing."

"She didn't call me I was there."

"If I were you I would work it out with
Steven."

"Mike did you hear me? I was there, so
Toni didn't call me?"

"I talked to Kelli that day and she told me
Steven invited himself to her table and hit
on her while she was eating. I guess that's
why he was hard on her, he wanted her for

himself. I'm glad she stuck him with the check."

"So, it was a chance meeting."

"I didn't want to tell you, but this jealousy has to stop."

"You really believe that?"

"Why not?"

"I saw her with my own eyes, so I'm not doing this out of jealousy."

"So you believe Toni, what did Steven say?"

"He hasn't because I won't talk to him."

"Are you sure you're not seeing more into this because of what Toni said or because you dislike Kelli?"

"Mike you need to leave her because she's going to hurt you." Sydney exclaimed. "Syd why are you trying to kill our friendship and my relationship with Kelli," Mike asked.

"I know what I saw."

"Stop being petty, I thought you were bigger than that."

"Mike, you said you didn't trust her and was in love with me."

"I was drunk and upset, so what did you

expect?"

"Is that all it take for you to tell another you're in love with her...never mind."

"Oh don't stop now you've already torn up our relationship. You are really good at running men off."

"I can't believe you said that."

"I think it's time to go, so are you coming or is your boy...oh yeah." Mike laughed

"Forget you Mike." Mike beat Sydney to the car and sulked until she got in. They rode home in silence.

That evening Mike was pacing back and forth in his room becoming more and more frustrated with each step. "Where is she?" Her voicemail came on, "Kelli I've called you eight times today and you haven't called back, is everything okay? I'm not upset just concerned. Please call or text me when you get this message." Mike sat on his bed and waited for the phone to ring. He started getting anxious again and picked up the phone to call her. His phone started ringing as soon when he picked it up, "Kelli, are you alright?"

"No its Luke and I'm fine, but are you alright."

"I haven't seen Kelli since Toni put out that rumor and I'm worried because we get married in a few weeks. Sydney's gone crazy and I'm just...man."

"Well I trust Syd because she wouldn't do anything to hurt you. Man the truth is in front of you."

"Kelli is not cheating on me and Syd is upset because she picked another dud."

"Steven is good for Syd and he called that trick of yours out the first time he met he."

"That's because he wanted her for himself and now he's mad because she said no."

"What show are you watching, because Kelli called out his name the morning he stayed over and Steven has treated Syd like a queen."

"That was a slip of the tongue because he was staring at her so hard."

"Mike, wake up, he was focused on Syd until old girl started with the insults."

"I gotta go that's Kelli on the other line." Luke yelled, "Wake up Mike."

"Hey babe, are you okay?"

"Yes, I went to the spa to get some of this tension from your friends out of my head."

"Get some rest and call me tomorrow."

"Is Sydney still dating Steven because if she is I'm not coming over anymore."

"No they broke up." Kelli got excited, "so he dumped her?"

"No, she dumped him because she says she saw you two together."

"She was there?"

"She said she was. Did you see her?"

"That's why I say this is messy because if she had seen me why not say something to me? All of this drama is giving me a headache."

"Well call me tomorrow baby. I need to go in here any lay down some ground rules for Sydney. She needs to learn to respect our relationship and not bring Steven in this house."

"Don't forget to tell her that he came on to me, so she'll leave him for good."

"If she goes back to him, she deserves whatever she gets."

"Calm down and don't let her go back to him."

Mike took a deep breath after he got off the phone. He decided to talk to Sydney before he lost his nerve. Mike was about to knock on Sydney door when she opened it.

"Mike, what you are doing?"

"I came to talk to you."

"Okay, come on in."

"I think after the misunderstanding the other night we should go downstairs."

"You were the one doing the kissing, not me and it happened downstairs."

"Okay we can talk in your room. I love Kelli enough to control your actions."

"Just not your."

"What did you say?"

"Nothing, what did you want to talk about?"

"Steven, my relationship, and a few rules until I move out."

"What Mike?'

"First, Steven can't come over or spend the night if Kelli is here because I don't trust him. Second, respect Kelli. You may be bitter because your dream man was a dud, but you can't lash out at sweet Kelli. Third because In love you like a sister I don't want you to have anything to do with

Steven because he's no good for you."

"Really, sop who made these rules?"

"Kelli had nothing to do with it."

"The relationship I have with Steven is my business."

"That's what I told Kelli, you're a big girl, so if you get hurt that's on you and I couldn't care less."

"I find it strange that your girl is concerned about my relationship with Steven."

"She cares about you, but you have so much hatred towards her you can't even see it."

"That chick hates me and me being with Steven drives her crazy for some reason, so Mike it's time for you to go Steven is on his way over."

"So you're going to give him another chance when he tried to seduce my woman?"

"You do it for Kelli. So why not hear his side."

"We've been together longer than two weeks."

"You are so silly, we were not serious, but now I think we should go to the next level."

"You are making a big mistake."

"unlike you I knew he was seeing other women."

"That proves something is wrong with you."

"No, I wanted to take it slow."

"He is not welcomed here."

"Yes he is."

"When are you going to stop being so easy?"

"Go to hell Mike."

"I'm waiting for you to open the door."

Sydney stormed out of the room and waited for Steven outside.

Chapter 5

Sydney had been sitting on the porch for twenty minutes when Steven pulled up. Steven walked up on the porch looking confused. "Is everything alright?"

"Yes."

"Then why are you sitting outside?"

"I got into an argument with Mike."

"About me right," Steven asked as he sat down next to Sydney.

"Yes, Kelli wants you band from the house and I'm not allowed to date you."

"Kelli said that not Mike?"

"Mike said that she cares about me and doesn't want you to hurt me."

"Baby, I have struggled on whether to tell you something since I met Kelli that night." Sydney feared Steven's next sentence, so she braced herself knowing that Kelli didn't lie. "The woman I was..." Sydney covered his mouth. "Steven we have not established anything because we were caught up in past relationships, so it doesn't matter. You had a past and I had a past, but now we are together, so starting today let's leave the past there because it doesn't matter."

"Wait I thought you were single?"

"I was but the man that had my heart kissed me and said he wanted to marry me a few days ago, so I was having second thoughts about you."

"I guess both of us had to clear up our past issues. Forgive me if I hurt you, but I have not flirted or had sex with another woman since the night I wanted to become exclusive."

"It's cool I didn't believe her anyway, but why were you there?"

"I wanted to see how I was going to handle a particular situation, because I wanted to be with you."

"Was it about your past?"

"Yes."

"Then I don't want to know about it."

"Sydney please let me tell you because I do not want to keep anything from you again."

"I only have one question, did you use protection with her?"

"I always used protection, because she wasn't my wife." Steven held Sydney's hand and asked, "Is there anything else?"
"No, I think we're ready to try this again."
Steven stood up and held out his hand.
"Hello, my name is Steven." Sydney smiled. "Hello, my name is Sydney."
"Would you like to go steady?"
"Yes I would." Sydney smiled and hugged Steven. "Well I have a meeting in the morning so I'll call you tomorrow. Let's make plans for a little getaway this weekend."
"Okay." They kissed. Sydney watched him as he walked to the car. He waited for her to go into the house before he got into his car. Steven drove away concerned about Sydney not knowing the truth. Sydney slept like peacefully.

Sydney awoke that morning feeling like a new woman, decided to relax today. She took a shower, put on a jogging suit, and completed her morning hygiene routine. Sydney rushed downstairs to cook breakfast. After she started cooking Mike walked in. "Good morning Syd, I see you followed the rules last night." Sydney ignored Mike as she continued to cook. "Rules, what rules does a grown woman have in her own house?" Mike did not see Luke in the kitchen and was shocked by his response. "Luke this does not concern you." Sydney thought she would get Luke riled up this morning, so he could Mike in his place since he was better at it. "I'm not allow to have Steven over or disrespect Kelli while he's living here."

"Mike you done lost your mind, man and Syd if you follow them you're just as crazy as he is." Luke looked at Mike. "Are you serious, obey my rules! I can't wait for Toni to get here, so I can tell her about this crap."

"Luke you need to stay out of this."

"Why, because Kelli is going to be upset. Man every decision she makes includes Steven, you know she wants to hit that or has she hit it already?" Sydney started laughing. "She's concerned about Sydney and doesn't want her to get hurt." Luke sat at the table with his plate. "Syd doesn't need that type of fake concern, she has us to protect her."

"Kelli is right about you guys, you're bringing me down mentally and financially.

"I have the same degree and opportunities as you, so I don't need you for a damn thing." Luke stated.

"Then why am I moving up in the company and you're still a Junior VP?"

"Because my girl didn't suck my way to the top."

"What does that mean?"

"Before you got your promotion Kelli was wining and dining Mr. Medlock a few times a week and his wife wasn't invited to the last meeting."

"That's what I'm talking about, Kelli was right you're not my friends."

"Who's not your friend Mike?" Toni asked as she walked into the kitchen. Mike stormed out of the kitchen. "What's wrong with him?"

"Kelli," Luke exclaimed. "Did he finally catch her?" She smiled hoping they had broken up.

"No, he believes her lies." Sydney said as

she set a place for Toni. "Have you talked to Steven?"

"Yes and we are a couple."

"No Syd you saw him with her."

"I saw him at a restaurant, not a hotel."

"But you know something is going on between them."

"No, I don't and if was in the past if there was something."

"He's cheating on you."

"We are not married and we were not in a committed relationship, so how did he cheat on me?"

"She got you there Toni," Luke said pointing his butter knife. "You do deserve better Syd."

"I kissed another dude while we were together and would..." Toni interrupted Sydney. "Kissing Mike has nothing to do with this."

"Wait, you kissed Mike? Syd, come on." Luke exclaimed.

"No, he kissed her, told her he loved her, and wished he was marrying her."

"He was drunk Luke, so it doesn't matter."

"I don't know Syd, men tell the truth when

they're drunk."

"Toni you have a big mouth. He had just gotten into a fight with Kelli, so that's the only reason it happened."

"And you believe that?"

"Yes Luke, why not?"

"Sydney I see you can't be trusted either. I was going to eat, but you make my stomach turn."

"Okay Mike, that was uncalled for. Syd you know Toni can't hold water."

"I didn't tell her, stop reading my diary."

"Your grown behind still writes in a diary, hell you are a virgin." Luke laughed.

"She's not a virgin or innocent." Mike exclaimed.

"How do you know Mike," Toni screamed, "was kissing the only thing that happened that night?" Kelli walked into the kitchen.

"Here we go again; all this ghetto drama is so annoying. Mike, why do you insist on wasting your brain cells with the likes of these people? Staci and her husband might be normal, but these three should be taken out back and shot."

"You stuck up b..." Luke grabbed Toni and

put his hand over her mouth. "Let's go Toni."

"I wonder if your wife knows how much time you spend with that trollop, while you have your nose in Mike relationship you need to work on your own."

"I wonder if Mike knows how much time you spend on your back, so your knees can take a break."

"That's it, Luke get out of my house!" Mike pointed to the door as Kelli clung to Mike. Luke and Toni left without saying a word.

"Did Steven say over last night baby?"

"Why does my man's actions concern you?"

"It doesn't, but I wanted to make sure you used protection or at the least protected your heart."

"Kelli she won't listen or take your advice because she envies what we have."

Sydney threw up her hands and stormed out of the kitchen as Kelli laughed.

Kelli followed Mike to his bedroom asking questions about Steven and Sydney. "Did he come over last night?"

"Who?"

"Steven."

"Yes."

"What happened?"

"I guess they talked. Kelli I have to go to work, so I'll see you tonight." Kelli plopped down on the bed. "What are you doing?"

"I'm going to chill here until you get home."

"No you're not."

"Why?"

"Because I can't protect you."

"I don't need you to protect me."

"I don't want you here and I'm not here because this is still her house too."

"Okay I'll leave."

"Call me when you're on your way home."

"Okay." Kelli and Mike walked out together. Once Sydney heard them pull off, she came out of her room. Sydney decided to go shopping for the unplanned weekend and wash this day out of her mind.

Sydney was writing in her diary about the events that happened that day. Staci called her to find out what happen after talking to Toni. Sydney had turned off her phone until she got home to avoid her friends. Staci called until Sydney finally answered "Hello."

"Sydney, where have you been?"

"Shopping."

"Does that mean you don't have to answer the phone anymore?"

"Yes because my loving friends will call me with a million questions."

"What do you mean?"

"I know Toni has called you."

"Well are you okay?"

"Yes I am. As a matter of fact, I'm waiting for Steven's call so we can plan a getaway for this weekend."

"Isn't he cheating on you?"

"No."

"So when is this getaway again?"

"This weekend."

"My dinner party is this weekend."

"Staci I don't really want to come to your dinner party, since Mike is going to be there."

"Sydney I can understand, so my door is open to you."

"Thanks Staci."

"I love you, so don't settle for Steven if he's cheating on you."

"He is not cheating on me, so I will enjoy him until I see something different."

"Be careful because you could get hurt."

"How am I going to get hurt if I am walking into the situation with my eyes open?"

"Because he is sleeping with other women and Kelli might be one."

"Mike and Kelli denied it, so I'm moving on."

"Promise me you won't fall for anything and let him hurt you."

"Okay, but he is not the one that's hurting me."

"You mean Mike?"

"Staci I have to go."

"Sydney we need to talk about this.

"No, we don't."

"Sydney, you know you're in love with him and you need to talk about this."

"Bye Staci." Sydney hung up before Staci could say anything.

Kelli met Mike at the house that evening.
They were arguing about Sydney in his
room. Mike walked into the closet to put
his suit up. "Mike did you hear me?" Kelli
yelled.

"Yes everyone can hear you."

"Well answer me."

"What Kelli?"

"Did Steven come over last night."

"I told you that this morning."

"Did he spend the night?"

"No, they talked."

"Where?"

"Outside."

"How long did he stay."

"I'm not sure."

"Was he in her bedroom?"

"No they were on the porch."

"Do you think thy got back together?"

"I'm not sure."

"Did he kiss her?"

"I don't...Kelli why are you asking me all
these questions?

"I want to help her because she can do
better."

"I know but she won't listen."

"I can set her up with this guy my daddy just hired."

"No, leave it alone."

"We have to do something to break them up."

"What you could do is give me a sneak preview of our wedding night."

"Mike, I can't believe you." Kelli stormed out of the house. Mike finished changing clothes and sat on his bed.

Sydney sat on her bed and started writing in her diary. After twenty minutes her phone rang again causing her to become annoyed. "If this is Toni, Hello," She said aggressively. "Hey baby, are you okay?"

"Yes Steven, I thought you were someone else."

"What's wrong?"

"My friends keep warning me about you because they are scared I'll get hurt."

"I understand, so I'll do everything in my power to keep that from happening."

"Thanks."

"Has your roommate done anything new?"

"yes but I don't have the energy to talk about him and Kelli."

"I understand," Steven said thinking about the weekend.

"Thanks." Sydney sighed.

"I want to take you to my beach house and have a long conversation about some things."

"I don't want to talk about the issues we've had over the past couple of weeks."

"Sydney, I've made a lot of mistakes in my past and I've made some major decisions about my future. Before we get too far along going towards our future, I want to talk to you about some things."

"I'm looking forward to it." Sydney felt relaxed. "I wish my friends would calm down."

"Well right now I'm the big bad wolf."

"But you haven't cheated on me, so why are they acting like this?"

"I look suspicious because of the restaurant, but since I told you everything we are going to be okay."

"I know."

"Without a doubt."

"Are you done with your ex?"

"Yes."

"Does she know it's over?"

"Yes, she came over yesterday and I made it clear."

"So she came over?"

"Yes, but without my permission and I did not let her in the house."

"Steven, please don't hurt me."

"Baby I... "hold on someone is ringing my doorbell." Steven walked to his front door and looked out of the peep hole, but did not see anyone. He opened the door and Kelli jumped out from behind the bushes, "Hi Steven darling." Steven quickly closed the door. "What are you doing here?"

"Steven, open the door so we can talk."

"You need to leave."

"I'm not leaving until we talk."

"Goodbye Kelli." Steven walked into the bedroom. "Now what was I saying...oh yeah. I've been waiting on a woman like you all my life, so I will not mess this up."

"You can stop blowing my head up. I said I was going to give you a chance."

"Woman just know I'm not letting you go."

"Well if you mess this up you don't have a choice."

"I refuse to do...what in the."

"Sydney let me call you back."

"Is everything alright?"

"I just heard a loud crash in my garage."

"Okay be careful."

"Bye." Steven hung up and ran into his garage.

Sydney was concerned about Steven but was quickly distracted by the knock on her door. She knew it was Mike and was not in the mood for his mess. "Yes Mike."

"Can we talk?"

"Come in and have a seat."

"I'm sorry for being so rude, but I think Kelli is right and you need to leave Steven alone."

"So you can in here per Kelli to help me?"

"Yes, Kelli is really concerned about you."

"She hasn't even been truthful to you yet she wants to help me."

"I see you believe that messy Toni when she tried to set her up. Did you know it was Toni that invited Steven there too?"

"Mike I'm getting ready to pack for a much needed trip, so I don't have time for this."

"Where are you going?"

"With Steven."

"Haven't you heard anything I said about him?"

"I don't believe you lying little girlfriend."

"You are so ungrateful," Mike yelled.

"Why," Sydney exclaimed.

"Because Kelli is trying to be your friend," Mike calmly said.

"No she's not. Mike we could never be friends."

"You are so petty. I can see you haven't grown up yet."

"I'm petty, your girlfriend lied on my boyfriend."

"I see you let that harlot Toni and I'm starting to worry about you, but then you can't make a whore into a housewife."

"I think it's time for you to leave."

"Enjoy your trick." Mike stormed out of Sydney's room. Sydney quickly called Steven to see if they could leave sooner buy his phone went straight to voice mail.

She sighed and fell back on her bed and cried.

Steven walked into his garage and saw that the door was closed. He looked around to see if anything was out of place. He looked on the driver's side of his car and saw a few boxes on the floor. He had been loading Kelli things up, so he could mail them to her. The boxes were the only things that had fallen, so he walked back into the house and locked the door. When Steven turned towards his room to call Sydney he bumped into someone in the dark hallway. "Steven, why did you pack all of my things?"

"Kelli, how did you get in here?"

"I came through the garage."

"I changed the co..." Steven remembered he had gotten distracted and forgot to change the code.

"Yes you change the locks on everything except the garage, so that lets me know you're not over all this goodness."

"Are you naked?"

"Steven, you know you can't resist me."

"Yes I can." Kelli rubbed herself against Steven. "Stop lying to yourself."

"Put your clothes on and leave before I call the police." Kelli held up his phone, "Then I'll call Sydney and let her know it's not over between us."

"That would only hurt you because she will tell Mike>"

"Mike won't believe a word she says." Kelli scratched Steven on his back. "Now how are you going to explain that to Sydney?" Kelli started laughing. "What is wrong with you?" Steven snatched his phone out of her hand and pushed her towards the door. "Leave," he yelled. Kelli gave him a cynical smile. "I'll leave but now you have to explain those scratches to your girlfriend." Kelli walked out the door laughing as she wrapped her coat around herself. Steven called Sydney after Kelli left. After three rings Sydney answered the phone. "Steve is everything okay?"

"Yes baby, but are you alright?"

"Yes, I was worried about you because it took you so long to call."

"Sydney, I'm okay."

"So what was it?"

"I guess the boxes in my garage didn't like the way I stacked them, so they fell over." He laughed. "I saw I missed a call from you, so what is going on?"

"Mike came in my room and wanted to talk after he apologized."

"Well that sounds promising."

"No it was not."

"What happen?"

"He wanted me to know that Kelli was just trying to save me from you."

"I am so tired of them."

"You're not the only one."

"Sydney, what I'm about to tell you will cause me to feel worse."

"What is it?"

"I can't take you to the beach house this weekend."

"Steven that's okay." Steven sighed with relief. "Steven would you like to go over Staci's house with me?"

"For what?"

"She's having a dinner party for us and I want you to come."

"Doug is going to be there?"

"Yes."

"Then I'm there."

"Great, it's this Saturday at six."

"Okay I'll see you then."

"Bye Steven."

"Bye beautiful." Steven and Sydney hung up. Steven was concerned about canceling the trip at the last minute. Sydney was wondering if Steven backed out of the trip because she was a not ready to have sex. They both fell asleep concerned about what the other was thinking.

Chapter 6

Toni and Luke were at her house plotting the break-up of Mike and Kelli before Staci's dinner party. Luke was pacing back and forth. Toni was getting annoyed with Luke, "Will you sit your over-grown behind down." Luke walked towards Toni. "Toni how can you sit there when our best friend is about to marry a succubus," Luke exclaimed. Toni laughed at Luke and crossed her legs. "Luke, that punk has belittled Syd and caused her unnecessary grief, so I don't care."

"Toni we are having dinner with them tonight and still don't have any proof."

"I know Luke but Syd text me, so she won't be there."

"Mike and Kelli will, so...why is Syd not going to be there?"

"She's going on a getaway with Steven."

"Toni what is wrong with our friends?"

"I guess the rational ones were infected by us, the irrational."

"I guess so, but what are we going to do to

save them?"

"Well Mike can fall head first in the deep end, but Syd is using her head."

"You're just mad at Mike because of the other day."

"Yes I am."

"Toni we can't let his dysfunctional behavior stop of from protecting him."

"I know but it feels good to say those things."

"Come on Toni let's get serious."

"I hired that PI a few days ago and I'm waiting to hear back from him or get some pictures."

"When did you get a PI?"

"After the restaurant because like Mike said we didn't have any proof."

"Good thinking, but she's going to be on her guard now."

"She's too conceited to be on her guard." Toni said turning up her nose at the thought of Kelli.

"But she's also wicked, so getting those pictures would help."

"Luke I got this."

"I bet you do." Luke smiled as he

embraced Toni and kissed her on her neck.
"I thought we were focusing on Mike and
Syd?"
"We are but I saw something on your
neck."
"Luke how are we going to help them when
we're sneaking around?"
"Toni, no one will ever think we are a
couple."
"What about Christine?"
"Didn't she put me out after putting a five
pound bag of sugar in my car?"
"You should've given her a ring."
"I told her I didn't want to marry her when
she moved in."
"But you let her move in."
"No I didn't she said she had been laid off
and didn't want to use up her savings, so I
let her move in."
"You let her be your maid."
"No, she did that and then she started
talking about having kids."
"Well you've been with her for over five
years, why not settle down and have a
family?"
"Christine quit her job and stop taking her

birth control so she could trap me."

"What?"

"Yes that's why she put me out six months ago."

"I still want to know how she put you out of your own house."

"Toni, after she destroyed my car I wanted to kill her, so to keep me out of jail I just left and gave her a thirty day notice."

"But she's still there." Toni said looking confused.

"I gave her three months to get a job and she had to be gone by the third month, but she said she's not leaving." Luke started pacing again. "What are you going to do?"

"I've been so wrapped up with Mike and Syd I almost forgot about these last few months."

"What are you going to do?"

"I talked to my friend from school and he's filing the eviction papers."

"What if she tears up the house after she gets the notice?"

"I'll sue her."

"I still don't understand why you didn't just give her a ring, heck she calls you every day."

"I'm not giving a ring to a woman that's not even ready to be a wife and I send her calls straight to voicemail."

"If you didn't think she was ready to be a wife you should've left her alone a long time ago."

"Toni we had an agreement and I was doing her a favor, so how is she going to nag me about something when the relationship was almost over."

"Luke every woman want's her knight in shining armor or in your case a man with a job and is as faithful as a puppy."

"We are supposed to be talking about Mike and Syd, not me."

"You're the one that keeps getting distracted."

"You keep distracting me, Toni go put on some clothes."

"This is my house and if I had known three months ago you would still be here I would have never answered the door." "

You should be happy that a man felt safe enough to cross your threshold, you man eating badger," Luke exclaimed.

"Badger...badger, is that all you have? Toni laughed, "You are so weak quick draw."

"You didn't complain while I was breaking your back last night."

"I must've been sleep because I don't remember."

"I'm your dream man and that's why your ass was knocked out last night."

"Well let's try it again, so I can see if you'll put me to sleep." Toni jumped up and ran towards the bedroom. Luke quickly followed.

Sydney was pacing in her room waiting for Steven. Toni called, but she sent the call to voicemail because she was not in the mood to talk to her. Sydney sat on her bed and taunted with the idea of calling Steven, but she knew he was working. She decided to write in her journal since her friends gave her a hard time about her diary. Sydney sat at her desk and wrote about her feelings.

Sydney was startled by her ringing phone. She quickly answered when she saw that it was Steven she, "Hi Steven."

"Hey babe."

"Are you on the way?"

"No, I have one more report to write." Steven was trying to surprise Sydney, but he felt bad about lying to her. He knew the scratches that Kelli put on his back would be too fresh for her not to suspect something if they had gone to the beach house. "I guess I have to be patient." She smiled, thinking about how great Steven was. "I'll pick you up in an hour and take you to my house so I can change."

"That sounds great." Sydney hung up so fast she didn't respond to Steven when he said, "Bye." She wanted to change clothes again. She had already changed three times, but she wanted to look great for Steven and shut Kelli up. Sydney decided she had to go to the mall.

Staci was enjoying her lazy day in bed with her husband since she didn't have to cook that morning because of the party. "Doug, why did you marry me?"

"You know why," he laughed.

"No, did you want to marry me?"

"Yes baby, I knew you were my wife when I first laid eyes on you in that little uniform." Doug pinched Staci under the covers. "Stop Douglas, you're so fresh."

"I know that why we had to get married."

"I didn't want my father to kill you."

"You mean kill us." Doug exclaimed.

"Doug if I had not gotten pregnant would you have married me?"

"Yes, but not as soon." Staci sat up in the bed. "Doug if you knew I was going to lose the baby..."

"Staci where is this coming from?"

"Mike and Sydney."

"What about them?"

"Mike is with a woman that is suspected of cheating on him but he won't believe anyone and Sydney is with a guy that cheated on her."

"What does that have to do with us?"

"If you found out I had cheated on you, would you have married me?"

"Staci, I loved you so much back then nothing could've stopped me from marrying you." Doug paused and rubbed his face.

"On second thought if you had faked being

pregnant or was pregnant by another guy I would've dumped you." Staci looked nervous. "Baby we know that would not have happened because you were a virgin and I was your first." Staci smiled and kissed Doug. "I love you Doug." Staci got up and walked into the bathroom. Staci had always way worried about Doug finding out the truth about her abortion. Staci always said she was a virgin during her first three years of college, but then she met the one or at least the one at the time. Staci fell head over heels in love with Cornell Louis, but he dumped her when she wouldn't put out, according to her. Two months later she started dating Doug. He was the good guy rebound because Staci was in love with Cornell. Doug fell in love with her after a few months and proposed, so they had sex. Cornell came over to Staci's apartment, which she shared with Toni, a week later. Staci had sex with Cornell, so he would date her again. A few weeks later Staci found out that she was pregnant and didn't know who the father was but she went to Cornell first. She called him, but he denied having sex with her and told her to never call him again. She called Doug and he told her to start planning their wedding. Staci wanted to have the baby but didn't know who the father was, so she knew she had to get one. Toni helped Staci plan a fake miscarriage before she eloped with Doug the day after finals. Staci was scared to tell Doug the truth but now he wanted kids and she hasn't been able to get pregnant. Staci knew she was being punished for her little secret in college. "Staci, are you going to come out of that bathroom so I can knock you up?" Doug yelled from the bed ax he got undressed. Staci eased out of the bathroom broken, but she knew that her secret had to die with her.

Christine is well educated and completely head over heels with the idea of marriage. Christine is the only one in her group of peers that hasn't been married or has a child. She's the first born and has always been a high achiever. Christine talks to her mother at least three times a week and can never avoid the same two questions; when are you getting married and why haven't you given me any grand kids? She has tried everything to get Luke to marry her or just get her pregnant because she knows he can provide her the lifestyle her girlfriends have. Christine is so consumed with the idea of marriage and having a child with Luke she tried to trick him into getting her pregnant. Her plan backfired and Luke told her to get out, but she refused. When Luke got home that evening she filled the tank of his Mercedes with a five pound bag of sugar. Christine walked into the house and begged Luke to forgive her, but he couldn't and slept in the guest bedroom. When he went to work that morning his car seemed to run out of gas before he exited his subdivision. Luke called his mechanic to tow his car, and then he called Mike for a ride to work. Luke got a rental car and drove home while Christine was at the gym and packed all of his clothes. Christine was heart-broken when she came home. Luke gave her a thirty day notice, but she didn't leave. After his first notice she sent him a congratulations text, but he ignored it. She sent a second one with a picture of an ultrasound, but he ignored it as well. She knew her time line was up to impregnate herself and put the baby on him. After the text messages of her being pregnant, he knew she was crazy, so he gave her a month to find a job and three months to get out but she didn't leave. Christine believes Luke is coming back after he calms down. She decided to attend the dinner party Staci was having, so Luke could see what he was missing. Christine was determined to get Luke back.

Chapter 7

Staci and her husband, Doug, were setting the table and discussing the seating arrangement. "Staci, why are you putting Toni next to Luke," Doug asked as he picked up the name card. "They are friends."

"Friends that argue constantly."

"It's all in fun for them."

"Well it drove me crazy in college and I'm sure it will drive me crazy tonight."

"You can handle it for a few hours."

"No I can't, so move the card." Staci moved Toni's card next to her.

"What about Steven and Syd?"

"They are not coming."

"I saw Steven yesterday and he said he would see me tonight."

"Are you sure because he and Sydney are going to his cabin this weekend."

"Call Syd and check." Staci pulled out her phone and called Sydney. Sydney was at Steven's house waiting on him to pack for his business trip. "Hey Staci."

"Hi Sydney, I need to ask a question."

"Yes."

"Are you and Steven coming over tonight?"

"Yes, I text you after Steven and I got off the phone.",

"I did not get the text." Sydney looked through her phone. "Forgive me Staci, I thought I sent it, but it's still in my drafts." They both laugh. "Okay Sydney I'll see you later."

Staci ran into the kitchen. Doug heard a loud bang and ran into the kitchen. "What are you doing?"

"I'm trying to make some more hors d'oeuvres."

"Why?"

"Because Sydney and Steven are coming."

"I told you they were coming when we did the count, but I didn't know they were coming together until yesterday."

"I don't remember you telling me that."

"I said a co-worker and his friend." Doug picked up the guest list. "See co-worker plus one." Staci breathed a sigh of relief. "I didn't know you were talking about

Steven."

"Who else would I invite around these knuckle head friends of ours, plus I wanted Syd to see what she was missing out on."

"I don't think she's missing out on a thing because he's a cheater."

"He's a what?"

"You heard me, a cheater."

"Was he married to Syd?"

"No."

"Then how was he cheating on her?"

"They were trying to get to know each other and he said he wanted to get serious, but he got caught with Kelli."

"Who is Kelli?"

"Mike's fiancée."

"Were they at Syd and Mike's place?"

"No. they were at a restaurant."

"What were thy doing?"

"Having lunch."

"Who told you?"

"Toni caught them at the restaurant and Mike told me what Kelli said."

"Toni is a bitter and angry man hater, so her distorted views can't be trusted."

"Toni is a reliable source and trusted

friend."

"How in the hell is that cheating, just because they had lunch?"

"Kelli denied it and said Steven tried to hit on her." Doug started laughing. "Steven is not that tacky."

"How do you know?"

"I've known Steven for years, he was with the same woman for a long time. After they broke up he never hit on a woman when we went out, so I thought he would be good for Syd"

"That doesn't mean anything."

"Yes it does because some of the places go are filled to the brim with beautiful..." Staci cut her eyes at Doug. "I mean he has woman hit on him and he never took them up on their offer."

"That doesn't mean he didn't hit on her."

"I would never set Syd up with a dude that can't control himself."

"Well you set her up with a dud this time."

"You just want Mike and Syd together and that will never happen."

"You're a man so you'll never understand true love." Staci stormed off into the dining room and completed the name card placement.

Doug cut on some jazz to lighten the event up. Staci was still fussing over the seating arrangement. "Honey you've been playing with that seating arrangement for over three hours, please leave it alone and get dressed."
"Doug I want everything to be perfect."
"Go get dressed then." Staci ran off to get dressed and Doug rearranged the cards to give him peace. Staci appeared less than thirty minutes later and the doorbell rang.
"I'll get it," she sang as she walked towards the door. "Hello Mike and Kelli."
"Hi Staci, you see overly cheerful today."
"Yes. I am celebrating all of my friends and their mates."
"Are you sure you haven't had too much wine already?" Kelli snapped. Mike squeezed her hand and pulled her towards the living room. H whispered, "Baby calm down." Kelli rolled her eyes at Mike. Doug greeted them in the living room. "Hey Mike, how are you?"

"I'm great Doug, this is my fiancée Kelli."
"Hello Kelli. It's nice to finally meet you welcome to our home."
"Thank you Doug." Kelli sat on the sofa. Mike looked around, "Are we the first ones here?"
"Yes you are Staci," said as she bounced into the room.
"Thank god, now I can have a drink and relax before that loud mouth Toni gets here." Doug laughed. "I know what you mean. Toni and Luke together require two drinks." Doug poured Kelli a glass of wine and Mike a glass of bourbon. "Mike one ice cube right?" Doug inquired from the bar. Staci walked out of the room to answer her phone. "Hello."
"Why are you singing," Toni asked. "I'm just excited."
"Well I had to pick up Luke so we'll be ten minutes late."
"Okay take your time." Staci walked into the living room. "That was Toni. She had to pick up Luke so they are running late." Kelli looked over at Christine, "Did you know Toni was picking you husband up?"

Mike quickly glanced at Kelli as if to say be quiet. "Christine when did you get here?"

"I just walked in a minute ago." Christine looked at Kelli puzzled.

"Well it's great to see you again." Staci walked over to Doug. "Please pour me a glass of white wine." Doug looked at her and shook his head as Staci joined the others. "Okay."

"I'm surprise Luke isn't here yet."

"Me too," Christine said looking around nervously.

"I'm sure it was Toni with her slow behind." Doug said.

"I wish he had called me because I know it was torture being with that barracuda." Mike said causing Kelli to snicker. "Toni is a miserable ghetto slut that can't get a man so she wants everyone else to be unhappy like her."

"I second that Mike, but Kelli you are out of line." Staci was uncomfortable, so she changed the subject. "Christine how have you been, I haven't seen you lately?"

"I've been working on starting my own business." She lied. "So Kelli how long have you been seeing Mike?"

"We're engaged, Luke didn't tell you?"

"No he didn't."

"Well he was at our party with Toni." Kelli said full of deceit.

"Congratulations." Christine turned towards Staci. "I need to call Luke to see when he'll be here."

"Toni called and said they would be late because she had to pick him up."

"Oh so she picked him up."

"Of course." Kelli smelled the opportunity to instigate and cause more trouble for Luke. "Was Luke not at home?"

I was not at home, Kelli." Christine smiled because she knew what Kelli was trying to imply, but Christine knew Luke stayed with Mike or got himself a room. "Oh, I just thought that it was strange that someone else had to pick up your man."

"Thanks for your concern, but I got it." Kelli became enraged but kept her cool because she knew Luke would be there soon.

"Why is it so quiet in here?" Toni walked in mouth first. "There's the ghetto loud mouth." Kelli stated "I second that." Doug said raising his glass. "Doug, I'm not going to let either of you talk about my friend like that." Staci said as she walked over to Toni. "If it quacks and walks like a..."

"Doug stop"

"I was just joking, baby," Doug hugged Staci as he nuzzled his nose on her neck.

"Y'all need to stop all of that because you have guest. Unless you're going to share," Toni laughed.

"Toni you just confirmed to my beautiful wife that I was right about you."

"What did I confirm?"

"That you are desperate, so thank you quack quack." Doug laughed and hugged Toni. Everyone was laughing except Kelli. She rolled her eyes and pulled Mike closer.

"Kelli, why are you pulling Mike so close to you, don't nobody want him."

"Well Christine needs to pull you closer to her, so Toni won't get you."

"What does Christine have to do with this,

she isn't even here."

"Yes she is, so Toni is the only woman here without a man."

"I am always at our gatherings alone because that's how I roll and I don't want Luke."

"Well that's good to hear." Christine said as she walked into the living room.

"Christine what are you doing here?"

"What's wrong with your wife being here, Luke?"

"She's not my wife," Luke turned towards Kelli. "Shut the hell up Kelli. You're always running your mouth." Luke walked towards Christine and asked, "What are you doing here?"

"Staci called me to see if I was allergic to anything and confirm my attendance."

"But that doesn't explain why you're here?" Toni whispered to Luke, "I'm okay but I think you need to take her outside and talk to her." Luke escorted Christine outside so they could talk. Well that was getting juicy." Kelli said sitting up. "You need to sit your little instigating behind down." Toni said to Kelli. "Toni you need to shut the hell up, you're the one that's always starting something. Kelli she's just lonely and miserable, so ignore her." Kelli smiled as she snuggles closer to Mike. "You're right Mike because all I hear is loneliness and jealousy echoing in the air." "How can anyone be jealous of a relationship based on lies and deception while dreaming of a love that will never be." Staci jumped up," Let's play this new CD I just got."

"Toni, go help Staci for me." Doug said as he looked at Mike in confusion. Everyone was quiet while listening to the CD.

Ten minutes later Luke walked in with Christine trailing behind him. "Syd and Steven are pulling up, so when are we going to eat?"

"I thought Steven and Sydney were not coming." Kelli exclaimed.

"Well I guess they decided to postpone that weekend getaway." Toni said to annoy Kelli. Doug walked towards the bar saying, "I'm surprised that Syd would do something like that."

"Like what?" Kelli asked in amazement.
"Spend the weekend with a man; because she's still a...you know."

Luke looked at Doug, "No we don't know."

"If you're talking about a virgin, man that ship sailed a long time ago," Mike blurted out.

"So y'all did have...I mean let's eat." Doug looked at Sydney as she walked in. "Doug she's slept with everybody, so he's just a notch on her headboard and just like the rest, he won't last long either."

"Mike, I know you're supposed to be her friend, but you sound like a real..." Doug saw the look on Staci's face and decided to change the subject. "You what I'm not as elegant as my wife, so I think I need to change the subject before I get upset."

Staci smiled, "Thank you baby." Doug decided to walk away from the situation, so he went into the kitchen and Toni followed him.

Doug sat at the kitchen table and tried to rationalize what he heard Mike say about Sydney. "I know," Toni said as she walked

into the kitchen and sat down. "Toni, I always though Mike was in love with Syd and he was her first, but I guess..." Doug was shocked. "I know Doug, but since he's been with Kelli, Mike has lost his mind."
"How could he talk about her like that, Toni that was a real weak move."
"I know and it's all because of Kelli."
"What does she have to do with Sydney's sex life?" Doug Stood up and to get a platter out of the cabinet. "Nothing, it's because she told Mike she's a virgin."
"Is Mike and Syd sharing more than a house?"
"No, she's jealous of Syd and has disrespected her so many times, but when Steven came into the picture it got worse."
"Is Syd like that sexually?"
"No, she's still a virgin, unless she and Mike did more than kiss the other night when he got drunk."
"When did they kiss?"
"Mike got drunk a few weeks ago; he kissed Syd and told her he was in love with her and wished he was marrying her instead of Kelli."

"What?"

"Yes I know he finally told her the truth."

"Mike refuses to admit he loves Syd because he's scared she doesn't feel the same way."

"But Doug he's with that tramp that's cheating on him and we are trying to break them up before Mike marries her."

"How do you know she's cheating on Mike?"

"I caught her and Steven at a restaurant together and they looked cozy."

"Toni, I set her up with Steven because of his character, so I know he's not playing Syd."

"The first night Kelli met Steven she was acting strange and he was so comfortable putting her in her place when she disrespected Syd."

"So that makes him a cheater?"

"Well she's sneaking around with someone; because that's not the first time I caught her at that restaurant."

"Steven was engaged and he broke it off less than a month before the wedding, so playing the field isn't what he wanted."

"Well I think that it's strange they were there together."

"It could have been a coincidence."

"I guess so because they didn't leave together."

"We need to focus on Mike because I've never seen him act like that." Doug rubbed his chin. "Is she cheating or do you think she's cheating?"

"She's cheating, but Mike doesn't believe us because we don't have any physical proof."

"Did you get a PI?"

"Yes a week ago, but Luke thinks it might be too late."

"Speaking of Luke, what's up with him and Christine?"

"They broke up six months ago house so he moved out."

"Why are you picking him up?"

"She put sugar and water in his gas tank."

"Well he can get that fixed."

"Luke is cheap and since she won't pay to get it fixed he refuses to buy a car or repair his."

"I need to get back so Staci can get the

food out." Doug carried out some more hors d'oeuvres. Toni sat at the table thinking. "Toni why are you in here?" Staci asked. "I was just thinking."

"What's wrong?"

"What is Christine doing here?"

"She's Luke's plus one, so where is Mister?"

"He couldn't make it." Toni said as she and Staci walked into the dining room. "Toni you need to leave these unavailable men alone because you always end up at events by yourself."

"I like it that way."

"you're just lonely and bitter, so stop lying because the only man you have is your pillow covered with warm tears." Kelli laughed as Mike joined in. "Kelli why are you always opening your mouth to say something you know nothing about?" Luke inquired.

"For the same reason you defend that lonely cow." Kelli looked at Christine. "How does that make you feel knowing you man is always defending another woman?" Christine started crying and ran outside.

Luke walked out behind her. Doug yelled, "That was the last straw with all these insults back and forth. I'm not going to let anyone disrespect my wife or my house again." Everyone apologized. Luke walked into the dining room without Christine. "Where's Christine," Staci asked. "She went home."

"Are you alright Luke," Toni asked."

"Of course." Doug looked up and said, "I'm ready to bless the food, so go wash your hands so we can eat." Luke rushed off to wash his hands.

Staci started the conversation, "So Sydney, why did you and Steven cancel your trip at the last minute?" "Mike has to take a flight tonight for business."

"Really," Kelli chimed in knowing why the getaway was canceled. "So what time is your flight?"

"That's not your business." Mike retorted.

"She's your friend, so you should be concerned about his actions."

"Kelli what did I say about my house, the next person is getting out." Luke walked back in and sat next to Toni. "Man what did I miss?" Doug looked up smiling at Luke, "Nothing man. Bow your heads. Lord we thank you for our friends that are like family and this bountifully dinner we are about to partake in. May this day of love and togetherness regain for evermore in Jesus name Amen. Now pass me some meat because I'm ready to eat." Serving utensils click off serving bowls as the food was passed around and for a moment, everything was quiet and seemed normal. "I'm with Doug. Staci the food looks great, you're an awesome cook." Staci blushed. "Thanks Luke." Staci stood up. "I just wanted us to get together and reflect on our lives together, sine we have so much going on and don't have the time we use to. Mike and Kelli you will be married in less than a month, so you'll start building your lives together. Sydney at the rate you and Steven are going, I'm sure you will be married soon." Kelli started coughing; which interrupted Staci's speech. "Kelli, are you alright," Luke asked.

"Yes Luke, I was just wondering why your

wife left so soon?"

"Did Christine leave?" Staci asked looking around. "Yes, right after Luke made her cry." Kelli exclaimed.

"Kelli I'm beginning to see why people don't like you, so if you utter one more lie or negative remark in my house your ass is gone."

"Come on Doug she was just concerned." Mike pleaded.

"No she wasn't, so we will start over having a pleasant conversation. Steven I haven't seen you in a while, how are things?"

"Doug everything has been great with my new company and since I've met Syd I know it's only going to get better." Mike and Kelli rolled their eyes, but knew not to say anything. "I didn't know you had your own company."

"Yeah Luke, I wanted to leave a legacy for my family."

"That sounds great. My future father-in-law keeps pushing me to venture out on my own, but I just can't see it."

"Yes, Mr. Mathews is big on starting up

your own company, so you'll have multiple streams of income." Steven stated as he winked at Sydney. "I didn't know you knew Mr. Mathews, so I guess the world is small after all." Mike said looking at Toni. Doug started getting excited about that fact. "Man, you had an awesome opportunity to get him as a mentor."

"Yea Doug, he's one of the best mentors in the business. I met him over four years ago and departed with a wealth of knowledge and a different view of the bigger picture." Steven looked at Sydney, "What was his motto?" The three men all in unison said, "The abundance of life, true love, positive relationships, and family determines your outlook on the future." The men laughed. "I guess I need to make that a daily affirmation." Luke stated as he looked at Toni. "I hate I missed the opportunity to be one of his mentees, but I was training for the position I have now." Staci rubbed Doug's hand. "That's fine because you're up for a major promotion." Doug smiled at Staci. "Yes I am and once I get in the door you can quit your job and become a full time mother." Staci smiled and looked a Toni, who knew her issue. "If you ever want a meeting with my daddy, just let me know." Mike felt calm again. "That great babe," he said before kissing Kelli on the cheek. "This is great and all but I want to talk about us and our plans for the future." Toni stated bluntly. Luke playfully pushed Toni saying, "Oh Toni you just want to be nosy." "What's new?" Doug laughed. "No I don't." Toni said, folding her arms. Since we are done with dinner, I think we should continue this conversation in the living room." Staci jumped up to lead the way.

Chapter 8

After everyone was seated in the living room, except Doug, who went to the bar, Luke stood up. "I guess I'll start first." Luke took a deep breath. "Christine and I broke up and tonight she tried to rekindle something, but I met someone else and I'm ready to marry her." Mike looked around in surprise. "So Kelli was right about you cheating."

"No, I was never married to her and I moved out over six months ago."

"That explains why you were at our house so much and I had to cook breakfast every morning." Toni was shocked at Luke's confession of marriage. "Luke, are you sure you sure you want to get married?" Luke looked at Toni and smiled as he said, "Yes." Kelli jumped up. "Don't do anything until after our wedding."

"Trick this isn't about you so shut up and sit down." Toni exclaimed. Kelli stood there with her mouth open. "Doug, are you just going to let her say that and not put her out?" Doug looked a Kelli with a grin of annoyance. "Yes because I agree and I really don't like you." Steven laughed. "Doug, I can agree with you on that." Kelli frowned and turned towards Mike. "Are you going to let them talk to me like that?" "We can leave if you want." Kelli wanted to get even, so she sat on the sofa and pouted. Everyone ignored Kelli. "Who is she Luke?" Staci asked. "You'll meet her soon." Luke said, smiling as he glanced at Toni. "I just knew you and Christine were going to get back together."

"I'm shocked that Luke said the word married."

"When you know you have the right one you don't let her slip out of your hands."

"You mean like you did in college," Mike sneered. Steven perked up," What happen in college."

"He was engaged to Toni," Staci laughed. Kelli to perk up, "You tow dated?"

"Yes, we did," Toni boasted. "Why is everyone so shocked?"

"Because you hate each other," Kelli replied. Luke walked over to Toni. "We don't hate each other, we just like to give each other a hard time."

"They acted the same way in college, so I never saw a difference." Sydney snickered. "When are we going to meet her?" Staci reiterated. Luke smiled, "Soon, real soon." Staci turned her attention to Toni. "Have you met her Toni, since you're the one that takes him everywhere?" Toni leaned back and held up both hands. "I plead the fifth." Doug looked at Toni. "I don't believe this, Toni is speechless."

"I know one thing the spirit of forever after is in the air." Steven looked at Sydney and smiled. "So what are you saying man," Mike asked appearing uneasy. Luke looked surprised, "I agree with Mike. Steven what are you saying?"

"I believe I've found the last woman I'll ever date." Kelli jumped up angrily, "You would marry her when you could have a quality woman." Kelli threw her hand in the air. "I can't believe you would settle for that bottom feeder." Doug slowly stood up. "Hold the hell up. Kelli you don't even know Steven, so why would you say that?"

Doug winked at Toni. "What...I." "You heard me. Do you know Steven personally?" Staci became nervous. "Honey I think we should leave it alone." Kelli knew she was about to expose her secret, "Mike your friends are rude and ignorant." Toni interrupted. "You are a slut and you've been cheating on Mike with Steven and that's why you're so upset." Mike stood up and looked around in disgust. "I can't believe you're in on this with them Doug."

"Mike, I'm not a fool. Either she is sleeping with Steven or has a strong desire for him because of her reactions. I think you've lost it man."

"Kelli doesn't know him, but because he cheated on Syd she thinks could do better."

"That's not what she said. She put Syd down not Steven, so you need to wake up and reset your common sense ability."

"Mike we are leaving and all of your friends are uninvited to our wedding." Kelli storms out and Mike runs behind her. Doug walked over to Steven. "Man I just have one question for you..." Sydney interrupted. "I know the truth and that's all that matters." Kelli confirmed what Sydney had already figured out and she didn't like it. "Sydney, Doug just wants to protect you because we don't want you to get hurt." Steven felt bad because he knew her friends were right. "I know how things look, but I'm not going to hurt Sydney. I really like her and knowing she has friends like you will keep me on my toes." Steven shook Doug's hand, "Doug, I promise I will not hurt Sydney."

"Why should we believe that you've already cheated on her, so why should we believe that you won't do it again?" Toni asked. "I did not cheat, but I struggled with my feelings for my ex." Steven looked at Sydney and took a deep breath. "I was tempted by her, but Sydney knew because she was still dealing with her feelings for her ex." Toni looked at Sydney puzzled. "As a man Steven I can respect that since I've been living with a woman for the past three months. I wouldn't go back to Christine for anything now but at one time I was weak." Toni walked over to Sydney.

"Syd you have to live with your choices, so if you choose Steven I'll support you. My focus is bringing down that slut Kelli."

"What can I do to support you guys?"

"Thanks Steven but we can't get you involved."

Luke I can get pictures, emails, and phone records if you want."

"So, you're saying you have access to those things?"

"No Toni, but money talks." Staci screamed, "Steven, were you having an affair with Kelli?" Everyone turned their attention to Steven. "I was with the same woman for almost four years and we were engaged for almost three years before I broke it off. I met Sydney a few weeks after I walked away from her. After I had been casually talking to Sydney for almost six months she invited me over to meet you guys. My three year anniversary with my ex was the night before and yes I had sex with her before her I had not been with a woman for almost ten years."

"Ten years, dude were you a monk?"

"I think it's commendable for a man to wait,

Luke."

"No Staci that's not commendable that's a drought."

"Steven why did you wait?"

"Toni, I was waiting until I met my wife and I thought I had met her, but I guess I just wasted my time."

"No you didn't because Sydney is still a virgin, so you'll have to wait until marriage. People don't do that anymore, so when they do get married, they compare every partner they've had with their spouse."

"Well I've never done that."

"Toni, that's because I was your first and will be your last." Sydney perked up from her funk. "Wait what did you just say Luke?" Luke kept his composure, "I said I was her first and that memory will be her last." Doug started smiling and patted Luke on the back. "Man gone admit it your back with Toni and I must say it's about time."

"So this is Mister and if he is its been longer than three months." Toni rolled her eyes at Luke. "Man you can't hold water."

"You can't either that's why it's so hard to believe you kept that secret, well at least all married men are safe now."

"Shut up Doug. You know I've never dat...Well slept with a married man."

"Everyone knows you were playing the field with unavailable men because you were waiting on me." Everyone started laughing. "Doug where is your recorder because this is the second time Toni's been speechless."

"I'm not speechless Steven, but I just realized Luke said he wanted to marry me."

"I'm so excited," Staci said as rushed over to the bar. "We need to celebrate this occasion and plan the wedding." Luke embraced Toni for the first since college in front of their friends. "We have to get through Mikes wedding first guys."

"Baby, you were uninvited to their wedding remember."

"I'm glad we were uninvited because I didn't like her."

"Doug we are going to support Mike; therefore, we are going to their wedding."

"You're right Staci, Steven I have to go."

"Are you still his best man Syd or is he using Luke?"

"He picked me Toni, but that could all change after what happened tonight." Doug started cleaning up so everyone knew what that meant. "Doug and Staci we had a great time, but Toni and I have some catching up to do. Love you Syd and Steven it's always a pleasure." Luke and Toni quickly departed. "I guess I can help you clean up Staci." Steven looked at Sydney so they could leave. "We don't need your help. Good to see you again Steven. Love you Syd bye." Doug rushed out of the room after he shook Steven's hand and hugged Sydney. "Sydney you and Steven should leave so you can talk about some things." Sydney hugged Staci after she escorted her and Steven to the door.

After Mike and Kelli left Staci's house they sat in the car for twenty minutes as Mike begged Kelli to let his friends come to the wedding. "I hate those ghetto fools you call friends." Mike was upset with his friends, but he knew why they didn't like Kelli, but because she was going to be his wife she came first. "Kelli, I need the best man. I already dropped Syd, so I can't drop Luke too."

"Mike those people don't deserve you nor do they deserve to bask in your happiness."

"What can I do to change your mind?"

"Never talk to them again."

"After we get married I'll walk away from the friendship, but I need them at the wedding."

"Is Sydney bringing Steven?"

"I won't let Syd come."

"I'll let your friends come on one condition."

"Yes to whatever it is."

"Let's go buy a house today." Mike didn't tell Kelli that he paid off the balance of the mortgage on the house he shared with Sydney with the bonus he got after his promotion. He did not want to buy a house until he was married because he knew Kelli would be upset. Mike was hesitant, but knew he had to give in to her demands.

"Where do you want to live?"

"I want my name on the mortgage contract or deed thingy."

"If that's what you want." Mike knew he couldn't buy her a house before they were married...Mike just realized he was marrying a gold digger and she was stupid. "Let's start looking next weekend because I want to get approved before we shop."

"Why would you do that?"

"I don't want you to pick a house that we can't afford."

"But you make six figures, so we can buy anything."

"Okay Kelli, we can start whenever you want to." Mike took Kelli home and it seemed like the longest ride of his life. When Mike entered the gate Kelli rubbed his legs. "I want a house like my daddy's." Mike shook his head because he knew he could not afford a house like that. "Okay baby, talk to your dad about the type of house you want us to get so he can help." He pulled in front of the house. Kelli jumped up as she yelled, "Thanks Mike." Mike drove away wondering if he was marrying the right woman as his thoughts drifted to the night he kissed Sydney. He realized he was jealous of Steven. He tried to shake it off, but he missed his best friend.

After Sydney and Steven left Staci and Doug they decided to go to his place, so they could avoid Mike and Kelli. Steven was sitting on the edge of the chair in his living room as Sydney lounged on the sofa. "Syd, what would you like to know?"
"Why did you lie about having to go on a business trip?"
"I was scared."
"Scared, Steven you said you would never lie to me again."
"I know but I was caught off guard."
"Steven I was calm because of my friends, but I knew you were lying about a couple of things."
"You said you didn't want to know about the past."
"Well if the past is going to affect our future we need to discuss it."
"Are you sure about that?"
"Yes, I'm positive because I can't take the lies."
"Kelli came over the other night."

"Why was Kelli over her," Sydney
exclaimed.

"I thought you were ready to hear the
truth."

"Okay I'm cool."

"She's my ex." Sydney had a feeling that
they had a past. "I know you knew she was
the woman I was seeing before you, so
stop trying to act surprise."

"I'm not surprised, but I thought she was
just an ex."

"I tried to tell you, but you didn't want to
hear the truth." Steven sat next to Sydney.

"I know that you were in love with Mike."

"What makes you think that?"

"After being around your friends how can a
person, not and Doug let it slip that you
had sex with him."

"We almost had sex, but I couldn't go
through with it, so what are we going to
do?"

"I want to keep moving forward, but it's up
to you."

"How can we move forward?"

"One day at a time." Sydney smiled at
Steven's response. "What were you doing

at the restaurant with Kelli?"

"I wanted to come clean with you, but because she had been cheating on me with Mike and vice versa I wanted to give her a chance to tell him first."

"Why didn't you tell me."

"Because you wouldn't speak to me and when you finally did you didn't want to know."

"True, so let's get back to the trip."

"Kelly came over and I wouldn't let her in, so she broke into my garage and scratched me on my back."

"Kelli broke in and scratched you, really?"

"When I told you something fell in my garage, it was Kelly." Sydney pursed her mouth in disbelief at Steven. "Syd I am not lying." Steven pulled up his shirt. "Steven I'm not having sex with you."

"I want to show you what Kelli did."

"Did you call the police?"

"No, because she walked out and said she texted Mike from my phone and I would have to explain that to you, I was a little scared."

"You still lied to me about the trip, so this

changes nothing."

"I was trying to protect you."

"No, you were trying to protect yourself."

"That's not fair, I believed you about Mike kissing you."

"That's different."

"How?"

"I don't know."

"Kelli will do anything to break us up because she wants me back."

"Then why is she marrying Mike?"

"If I were to tell her yes, she would drop Mike so fast his head would spin."

"Then why not take her back?"

"I don't want her Syd, I want you." Syd blushed. "I want you to Steven."

"Are you sure?"

"Why would you ask me that?"

"I wanted to tell you about Kelli since that night, but I was scared I would lose you to Mike."

"Why would you lose me to Mike."

"Because he's in love with you."

"Mike thinks I'm a whore."

"No he does not. He just wants to have an excuse to give him peace, about not being with you."

"The only reason he supports Kelli's stupid request is because he does not want you with anyone else."

"That's crazy, have you heard the things he's said about me."

"He does that to keep his mind off the truth."

"Whatever. I don't want Mike for two reasons; one is you and the other is how he disrespected me."

"Sydney are you a virgin?"

"Why?"

"Because I want to know."

"Well if we get to that point you'll be the first to know." Steven pulled Sydney closer to him and kissed her passionately. "I didn't mean tonight, Steven," Sydney mumbled through kisses. Steven slid his hands over her shirt, causing Sydney to moan and pull him closer. Steven jumped up, "I think we need to stop." Sydney wiped her lips and sat up. "Thank you Steven." He kissed her on the forehead. "Would you like for me to take you home," Steven asked as he searched for his keys.

"I think it would be best."

"Yeah you're right." Steven and Sydney rode in silence. When Steven pulled up in the driveway he, got out and opened Sydney's door. They walked to the front door. "Sydney, I really like you and I would like to build a future with you." She smiled and hugged Steven as she gently kissed him on the cheek, "Ditto." Steven smiled and walked back to his car as she entered the house.

Chapter 9

The following week Sydney walked into the kitchen and saw Mike sitting at the table fumbling with his coffee cup. Sydney wished that Mike's business trip was longer. "Good Morning Mike."

"Morning Syd."

"Would you like anything to eat?"

"Syd can we talk?"

"Mike, I don't want to fight."

"No it's not that, I just want to talk."

"Okay."

"I miss what we had and after being gone for a week, I finally realized we've lost us. Syd I miss you." Sydney thought about what Steven said about Mike being in love with her. "Is everything alright?"

"Yes, I just miss my best friend." Mike smiled. "Will you forgive me for everything I've said or done to hurt you?"

"I forgive you." Sydney hugged Mike. "I know you're under a lot of pressure, so I pray everything is alright."

"You know me so well. I'm not sure if I'm

with Kelli because I love her or to prove a point." Sydney became uncomfortable because of her conversation with Steven about Mike kept popping up in her memory. "Mike you asked her to marry you before all of this mess started."

"I know, but I wonder if you guys are right."

"Mike, she just rubbed a few of us the wrong way."

"Yeah, but I've known you guys most of my life, so why would you have ulterior motives?" Mike stood up. "I've made a mess of things and now Kelli wants to buy a house, but I used my bonus to pay off this house. Syd I need help."

"You did what?"

"Kelli wants to buy a house before we get married and I don't want to." Sydney knew Mike let that slip, so she pretended as if she didn't hear it. "Tell her no."

"If I do that she won't let you attend the wedding." Sydney walked over to Mike.

"Do you hear yourself?"

"What?"

"She's running your life and dictates your

every move."

"But she's the reason I've advanced in my career and I'm on the right track."

"But are you happy?" Mike ignored the question. "Mike, you earned that position."

"No I didn't, her father's hand shake opens doors."

"But your ability keeps you there and your portfolio influenced that promotion." Mike was so confused. "Mike, you fell in love with a strong and controlling woman; which is a struggle, but I will support you."

"But what if I'm wrong and Toni is right?"

"You just have cold feet."

"Syd I have no idea what I'm doing."

"Ask yourself if you really want to spend the rest of your life you've spent the past year."

"You're right, so what happen to you and Steven?"

"We decided to take it slow."

"So, are you okay with that?"

"Yes, it was mutual."

"Well I wish you the best and I would like some bacon with my eggs." They laughed as Sydney prepared breakfast.

Mike and Sydney were laughing as if the past few months never happened. Kelli walked in to hear the laughter and became angry. "So this is how you decide to betray me?" Mike was shocked. "What are you talking about?"

"You're sitting here laughing and talking to the enemy. Mike, how could you?"

"Kelli we were just talking over breakfast."

"But she hurt me the other night, so how could you forgive her?"

"I asked her to forgive me for my behavior."

"Why would you do that, you haven't done anything wrong."

"Yes I have Kelli."

"What could you have done?"

"I wasn't a true friend and because of our journey, I could've been a better friend to Syd."

"But she deserves what she gets by being so easy."

"I don't know why I said she was easy." He felt silly at that moment. "Because she is."

"No, she's not." Mike gave Sydney a look of sincerity. Sydney mouthed "Thank you."

"I've never seen Syd with a man in this house or spend the night anywhere, so she must be good,"

"If you say so, but I'm ready to look at houses." Kelli turned up her nose up at Sydney but knew she had to walk a fine line today. Mike looked at Sydney, "Have and awesome day."

"Thanks Mike, I hope you guys enjoy your day as well." Kelli rushed out of the kitchen, so she could avoid responding. Mike embraced Kelli when he walked into his bedroom. "What are you doing Mike?"

"Embracing my woman."

"Why?"

"Because I love you and I missed you."

"I'm not giving you any."

"Kelli, I'm not trying to have sex with you."

"Then what are you doing?"

"I'm trying to show you some affection."

"Did you have sex with Sydney last night?"

"No, why would you say that?"

"You're acting strange."

"In less than two weeks we will be married and I realized, we don't show affection towards one another."

"I just know that will lead to sex because, I desire you Mike."

"Are you sure?" Kelli embraced Mike and gave him an arousing kiss. "Mike I am weak for you, so I have to be careful." Kelli knew she had to refocus her hold on Mike's mind. "I have self-control because I respect you."

"Mike that's easy to say, but in the heat of the moment we might slip." This was a true statement but Kelli used it to play Mike. Mike knew it would be hard to control the passion burning within him, but he desired to have an intimate relationship with his future wife that was not based on sex.

"Come on Kelli let's look for our home." Kelli jumped up and rushed downstairs.

The car was quiet until Mike pulled into the driveway of the first house. "I hate it," Kelli exclaimed.

"Why?"

"It doesn't have a gate."

"Kelli this is our first home, so let's be realistic."

"You got that big bonus after your

promotion so we can put more down." Mike had not pre-qualified for a loan or told Kelli what he did with his bonus yet, so he became nervous. "Baby let's just look at the house, since she's here and then you can tell her what you want."

"We can tell her it's not what I want."

"I think we need to look at this one because I like it."

"Are you trying to back out of our deal."

"Kelli it's my wedding too, so if my friends not there neither am I." Kelli was shocked.

"Mike what has gotten into you?"

"Kelli, I love you, but I'm going to be your husband, not your child."

"Forgive me I was just focused on what I thought was best for us."

"Let's look at the house." Kelli knew something was different about Mike and knew what she had to do to fix it.

Sydney was working on the final phase of her make it or break it project when the doorbell rang. She wanted to ignore it, but it could be important. Sydney ran to the door and opened it without asking who was there. When the door flew open Sydney stepped back in awe. There was a chef standing there. "I'm here to prepare your lunch." Sydney stepped out of the way and allowed him and his entourage inside. "Ma'am where is your kitchen?" Sydney closed the door and led them to the kitchen. Sydney knew Steven had done this since she's been too busy to meet him for lunch. Sydney went back to her work.

Luke drove by his house to if Christine was still living there or if she destroyed it after the eviction notice. To his surprise the house seemed empty. He parked on the street and walked around the house to be sure it was safe before entering. Luke opened the back door and the lights were off. His cell phone rung and startled him.
"Hello."
"Did she leave?"
"I think so."
"Are you in the house?"
"Yes."
"Well do you see any of her stuff?"
"No, but I'm still looking."

"You are so slow."

"I had to make sure she didn't jump out and stab me in my chest."

"Stop dating crazy women and you won't have that issue."

"But I'm in love with you." Luke laughed.

"Real funny, the locksmith just pulled up."

"What lock smith...where are you?"

"Sitting outside your house."

"Toni, what are you doing here?"

"I wanted to get your locks changed, so you can move back in."

"Toni you didn't even know if she had moved."

"Yes I did. I paid your neighbor to let me know when he saw a moving truck pull up."

"When did she move?"

"Wednesday."

"Why didn't you tell me?"

"I didn't want to be all in your business."

"So what are you doing now?"

"I'm helping you."

"Toni you're a sick woman."

"But you love it, so let's christen your house."

"Toni I'm selling this house."

"Why?"

"I spent five years of my life in this house with her and two of those we lived together." Luke paused. "Toni I want to start a new life with you, so I'm not moving back in here."

"Luke, you make me sick."

"Why?"

"You're being all sensitive and I wanted to do you on the living room floor, but now that just seems wrong." Luke started laughing. "Toni you're crazy." Luke walked out to the car as the locksmith changed the locks on the doors. "Luke my apartment is not big enough for both of us."

"I know and that's why I want us to get our own place." Toni was speechless. "Toni I want us to have a simple and quick wedding with our close friends and your grandmother."

"What about your parents?"

"They gave up on me when I didn't take over the business and my brother let it go under." Luke looked up into the sky as he reflected on his parents. "How long has it been?"

"Over fifteen years, they didn't want me to go to college, but my grandfather did and he set up a trust fund for me to go."

"I've never met your grandfather."

"He died during my first year of college while I was on summer break."

"That's right I met you during your sophomore year and I was just an innocent freshman."

"I don't know if I would say innocent because you lied to me about being a sophomore."

"Well you were dumb enough to believe it."

"I didn't care because you came into my life when I needed you the most."

"Why did you dump me then?"

"Toni you cheated on me."

"When we were always together."

"Rita Jones told me she caught you at Cornell Louis's house trying to sneak out."

"I was helping...Okay she caught me but I never had sex with anyone but you in college." Luke looked at Toni and paused. He decided to get in the car with her. "Who was having sex with him?"

"What?"

"Was it Staci or Syd and I doubt it was Syd."

"Luke please let it go."

"Is that why she married Doug so quick and faked a miscarriage because she didn't know who the father was?" Toni sat there in utter shock. "Who told you that?"

"I'm not stupid."

"I knew they got married because she was pregnant." Luke cut the air conditioning down in the car. "I also thought it was strange that she didn't go to the hospital after the miscarriage and it happened on their wedding night." Toni was speechless because it was if someone had told Luke, but no one knew but her and Staci. "Why would you think that?"

"Since we've been back together, I've realized how much talk you are and Staci has changed."

"We all change with time."

"Yeah, we do, but Staci was uncomfortable when Doug brought up kids the other night."

"Infertility is a serious thing."

"If that was an issue, how did she get pregnant in college?"

"I don't want to talk about this anymore."

"Okay, but I think it was foul that Staci didn't speak up when Rita told me you were cheating on me with him and she knew it was her."

"Staci didn't know who told you."

"Why not when she was standing next to her?"

"Staci was there?"

"Yes and confirmed that whole story."

"Why would she do that?"

"To protect herself."

"But she knew what our break up did to me, she could've at least told me."

"It's the past but I just thought you should know."

"Does Doug know because in college you were close." Luke sat back. "I told him she faked the pregnancy, but he didn't believe me and we stopped hanging out." Luke shook his head. "We fell out because Staci was an undercover ho."

"Doug was her first." Toni exclaimed.

"No he wasn't but y'all can believe that lie

she tells herself and those around her."

"How do you know?"

"Staci and I started together remember and Doug was a transfer, so by her junior year she was an angel again."

"I don't get it."

"She fell head over heels in love with Cornell and he never respected her so she changed her image to get him, but once he hit it he was done."

"And she has a nerve to check me." Toni began to getting upset and pulled out her phone. "What are you doing?"

"I'm going to call her," Toni exclaimed.

"Why when you can watch her lies unfold as she tries to keep it together. Doug is going to find out, so she'll need your support."

"How can I be there for her?"

"Just like you were in college, because you helped her scheme on Doug and you reaped the repercussion of that deceit."

"You're right, I never thought about how much that would hurt him."

"You were young and thought you were helping your friend, but you better not deceive me."

"I wouldn't do that."

"All of our friends are caught up in deceit right now."

"Well that's just Doug and Staci.

"No, Sydney knows more than she's willing to let on about Steven and Kelli."

"Why would she do," Toni sighed, "to protect Mike."

"Bingo and that's why I haven't confronted her about it."

"But if she has proof we need it to stop the wedding."

"Toni it must be something that will devastate him. Remember what happened to him a few years ago."

"Okay our friends are messed up, so let's talk about something else."

"We will have the bachelor's party over here and you better not do a drive by."

"Luke I wouldn't do that."

"Whatever, here comes the locksmith."

"I'll pay him, so you can go plan your stupid party."

"Would you like to get something to eat?"

"Yes," Toni said as she playfully pouted.

An hour after the chef Steven walked into Sydney's office with flowers covering his face. "Would you have lunch with me beautiful lady?" Sydney was a little startled because she did not hear Steven walk in. "Yes sir, I would love to be in your company for lunch." Steven escorted Sydney to the deck where they enjoyed a romantic meal and peaceful day.

Doug was concerned about Staci not getting pregnant, so he decided to go to a fertility doctor. He knew he partied hard in college, so he wanted to be sure he was not the cause of their issue. She was the first girl he had unprotected sex with; because she would be the last since she was a virgin he knew she was safe. Doug would rush home to get the mail every day until the letter came. When he got the letter he was scared to open it because he knew how much Staci wanted kids. He thought since Mike was getting married causing Staci to be in a better place he would open the letter, so he could give her the bad news. After he read the letter he

was heartbroken. Doug shredded the letter
and tried to put it out of his mind.

Chapter 10

Luke and Doug were setting up for Mike's surprise bachelor's party. "Doug I can't believe Staci let you help me do this."

"I know, but then she doesn't know where I am."

"You know Toni is going to tell her."

"Yep but it's easier to ask for forgiveness." The men laughed. The doorbell rang.

"Who's here this early?"

"You better hope it's not Staci." Luke laughed as he walked towards the front door. "Hey Steven, what's up?"

"Syd said I should come over and give you guys a hand."

"Doug you can come out, it's not Staci."

"He lied huh?"

"You know it."

"Hey Steven, it's good to see you."

"Better me than Staci?" Luke and Steven gave a high five and lauded as Doug stood there looking goofy. "Steven how are you going to throw me under the bus like that?"

"I didn't throw you under anything, but I am

enjoying you squirm." The men laughed.

"How many strippers did you hire Luke?"

"Doug you must be crazy if you think I hired strippers," Luke said, picking up a flyer, "because I only needed one for whipped Mike."

"Is this who I think it is?"

"Yes sir," Luke exclaimed.

"Who is it," Steven asked.

"It's Mike's favorite stripper," Luke smiled. Doug patted Steven on the shoulder. "Man he was so in love with her we thought she was going to get every dime he had."

"If that the case, why would you have her here?"

"So Mike will slip up and cancel the wedding."

"If we can get Mike to hit old girl the wedding is off and my boy will be saved."

"What if Mike doesn't care about Kelli's past?"

"The guy you see isn't Mike. Kelli got him after a bad break up, so he was weak and wanted to be loved."

"They have been together for two years, so he must love her."

"Mike is confused and it's my job as the best man to unconfused him."

"I just think you're headed for trouble."

"Steven, you have to understand when it comes to Luke's friends he will do anything to protect them." Doug thought about the night Luke warned him about Staci. "Even if it means losing them," Doug said emotionally.

"Man stop being sensitive and get the rest of the liquor out of my trunk." Luke gave Doug his keys. "Steven would you go up the street and het the wings?"

"Yeah."

"Let me call them again to see if they are ready yet." Luke walked into the kitchen to get his phone. Steven decided to help Doug bring the liquor into the house. Doug was staring at nothing and seemed to be in deep thought.

"Hey man I came out to help you with the liquor." Doug jumped. "Man I just have a lot on my mind."

"You want to talk about it?"

"Man it's nothing, let's get drunk and have some fun." Luke walked into the garage.

"Man I think they messed up my order, so I'll go up here to get the wings and Doug you can pick up Mike."

"What am I supposed to say?"

"I had a pipe that burst at my house, so you're picking us up for the celebration tonight."

"I thought it was a surprise?"

"It is, but we have to get him over here without him suspecting anything."

"What?"

"Doug you pick up Mike and then come here, but I'll call him and tell him why so it won't look suspicious." Steven laughed, "I think Doug has a lot on his mind." Luke shook his head, "No he's been like this since college, dude can't lie about anything."

"Man that was one time."

"One time was all it took."

"More college stuff huh," Steven laughed. Luke called Mike as he walked out the door. Doug put the liquor out and realized there was no ice in the freezer. "Steven can you go get some ice?"

"Yeah man, but what about the people

coming over?"

"They are parking at the club house and walking over."

"Doug I mean who's going to let them in?"

"Oh, they won't be here until six thirty, so we can get Mike here by seven."

"Luke was right about you man."

"What?"

"You can't lie, don't mess this up for Mike." Steven grabbed a box from Doug. "I'll call Luke and tell him to pick up the ice and you go get Mike because it's already after six." Doug rushed out while trying to call Luke. Steven continued to set up the liquor.

When Doug pulls up to Mike's house he saw him and Kelli on the porch. "Why are you here Doug," she yelled. Doug got out of the car and took a deep breath. "I'm taking my friend out to eat to celebrate his last day of being single." Kelli pursed her lips. "Are you going to a strip club?"

"Kelli I have a wife, so Mike isn't going to do anything I can't do."

"What about Luke?"

"That's why I'm going, so you won't have

anything to worry about."

"You're going out to eat and no strip clubs."

"No strip clubs, I promise." Kelli smiled and kissed Mike on the cheek. "Have fun guys," she said as she rushed off to her car. Mike looked at Doug. "We are going to a strip club right?"

"No Mike. You are almost married."

"I'm not married yet and Luke is my best man, so I know we are going to at least one club."

"No we are not."

"Good and since I know you can't lie I feel better."

"You don't want to go to a strip club?'

"No, but I know Luke."

"Well lets go pick him up."

"I'm glad you're coming, so he will be calm." Doug was about to burst so he didn't say a word as they drove off.

Luke started drinking when he got back home. "What time is it Steven?"

"Ten minutes to seven."

"Let me call Mike and see what's taking so

long." Luke turned down the music. "Everybody be quiet, I'm about to call Mike." Luke called Mike instead of Doug because he knew Doug would mess something up. "Where y'all at man," Luke exclaimed. "Doug is driving like an old lady, but we just turned into your subdivision."

"Okay, I'll be ready when you get here."

"Luke you're never ready when someone is picking you up."

"Just park and come in, I'll be ready in five minutes." Mike jumped out the car annoyed with Luke, but because Doug drove so slowly he knew why he wasn't ready. Mike opened the door, "Luke."

Luke walked towards Mike. "Come on and have a seat."

"Luke lets go." When they walked in Steven cut the music on and the other guys came out shaking Mike's hand and congratulating him. "Surprise Mike this is your last day as a single man party." Mike looked back at Doug. "I thought you said we were going to eat." Doug pointed towards the kitchen. "We went out to get some food and invited a few of the guys over, so we can eat." Mike shook his head and walked over to the bar. Luke told the bartender to take special care of Mike. He wanted Mike to be ready for his special treat. Steven walked over to Mike.

"Congrats Mike."

"What are you doing here?"

"Luke invited me by way of Sydney, I hope it's okay."

"It's cool because these guys tricked me, so I'll make the best of it."

"Congratulations Mike."

"Thanks." Steven walked off as Mike pulled up a bar stool. Everyone was drinking, talking crap and, eating.

Luke got a text from Honey, so he ran outside and escorted her in. He took her to the guest room, so she could get dressed. Luke let Steven and Doug know that Honey was there. Doug and Steven got all the guys in the living room. "What's going on?"

"Luke wanted us to get the guys in here to watch a flick."

"I told him Kelli didn't want me doing

anything enticing."

"If you don't get you whipped butt up, look I put a chair over here for you so you can turn around if it's too much." Mike sat in the chair Luke gave him and folded his arms. After five minutes the music changed and Honey came in. Mike's mouth dropped and he couldn't move. Honey had the guys yelling and Mike in complete awe. After ten minutes Mike jumped up and ran into the guest room. "Mike, where are you going?" Luke walked down the hall and knocked on the door. "Kelli said no strippers."

"That's not a stripper that's Honey."

"Luke please, I love Kelli." Luke walked into the living room. "He's not coming out, so Honey, you can go." The guys booed. "Hey y'all got free liquor and food, so be quiet." Honey tapped Luke on the shoulder. "Yeah."

"I don't mind dancing for the guys."

"If you want to dance, go on." Luke walked down the hall to get Mike out of the room. After twenty minutes Honey stopped dancing. Five minutes after she stopped everyone left except Steven and Doug.

Mike came out of the room when the noise died down. "Congratulations Mike."

"Thanks Honey."

"Don't worry I won't do anything you don't want me to." Mike wanted to run but his feet would not move. Luke walked over to Mike and patted him on the back. "Thanks Honey but I think Mike is a little scared."

"I don't bite Mike unless you want me to." She smiled and walked out the front door.

"Doug I thought you said you wouldn't do anything that Staci wouldn't let you do," Mike barked.

"I didn't, but I will watch a flick and go to the strip club every so often." Doug and Luke laughed. "I guess you're going to run and tell Syd," Mike said to Steven. "Why would I do that?"

"To make me look bad."

"I'm a man Mike, so I don't play silly little games." Steven walked into the living room and started cleaning up. "Mike, the party is over so you can call Kelli and let her know you didn't do anything out of order."

"I just respect my woman."

"Good night." Mike went to bed while the guys cleaned up.

Luke had set the timer for the coffee maker, so the guys could get a fresh cup in the morning. Mike was sitting at the kitchen table with a cup of coffee. Luke walked in. "Hey Mike you ready for the big day?"

"I'm nervous."

"That's normal."

"I know but I put a bid on a house that Kelli doesn't know about yet."

"Mike, why are you so scared of that women?"

"I just love her so much that I want everything to be perfect."

"That's what men do when they are in love, so I'm here for you."

"Thanks man."

"Where is everybody?"

"Doug and Steven went home around six this morning, but they'll be back before the limo gets here."

"Why were they here so late?'

"They had to sleep it off."

"Steven was drinking?"

"Yes, just like the rest of us."

"Oh, where's Syd?"

"She stayed with Toni last night."

"Why?"

"Because they are women, hell I don't know. Why are you asking about Syd?"

"I was just wondering."

"Well you need to get dressed."

"I will, but let me see the rings one more time."

"What rings?"

"The wedding rings."

"Mike I don't have the rings."

"I didn't give them...Doug picked me up."

"So what are you saying?"

"I left the rings at my house."

"Mike you need to get dressed, so we can pick up the rings before we go to the church."

"What time is it?"

"An hour and forty-five minutes till you say I do."

"Man when is the limo coming?"

"In an hour, so get dressed and we can get the ring drive back here in time for the limo" Luke called Doug and let him know what happened. Mike and Luke rushed out the door. Steven was pulling up as Luke backed out. Luke jumped out the car and told Steven what happened, so Steven went inside to let the other guys in.

Luke and Mike were running behind because Mike took so long to get dressed.
"How could you forget the rings?"
"I didn't want to lose them."
"That's why I told you to give them to me a week ago."
"I didn't trust you, so I kept them."
"You didn't trust me," Luke exclaimed.
"Man you know you hate Kelli."
"Yes but I'm not going to make you suffer."
"Well I..."
"Was being silly, now were running late because of you."
"Call Syd, shell know where I hid the rings."
"Syd is at Toni's house remember."
"Why is she over there, is she coming to the wedding?"
"I think so, but Toni lives further away

than I do."

"Syd is tripping."

"What, why are you focusing on Syd?"

"She should be at home."

"She was trying to avoid Kelli. Mike, today is about you stop worrying about Syd." Luke pulled up to the house and Mike took his time getting out of the car. "Man hurry up!" Mike picked up a package addressed to him as he walked in. Mike opened the package as he walked to his room. Mike got the rings and tucked the package in his pants. He ran to the car and Luke rushed to the church.

Mike and the groomsmen were standing at the front of the church as Kelli walks down the aisle. Toni leaned over to Sydney. "Mike looks scared."

"He's just nervous. He put a contract on a house she hasn't seen yet."

"When is he going to tell her?"

"After the honeymoon I hope." Sydney snickered. "I hope so or hell never get any." Toni laughed. Steven leaned over. "Will you two stop whispering and pay attention, because Mike is about to run."

"No, he's just nervous."

"Then why is he looking around like he's trying to find the nearest exit?"

"If I was marrying that evil witch I would be looking for an escape too."

"Stop, you guys." Sydney laughed and was hushed by someone in front of them. Kelli reached the front of the church. "Who gives this woman to this man?" Mr. Mathews proudly said, "I will." Kelli was smiling as Mr. Mathews shook Mike's hand and whispered something in his ear. Luke leaned over towards Mike. "Are you okay man.?"

Mike said, "Yes," after clearing his throat. Mike took a step to face the crowd.

"Before we go any further I would like to say something." The Pastor tapped Mike on the shoulder, but he ignored him. "Kelli refused to have sex with me before we got married." A few people mumbled in agreement and Kelli smiled at her parents. "She came between me and my best friends, Sydney forgive me." Mike turned towards Luke. "Man I should've believed

you and Toni, but now I have proof."
Everyone was trying to figure out what he
was doing. Sydney whispered, "Toni what
did you do?'

"Nothing, I don't know what he's talking
about." Toni looked puzzled. Mike walked
towards Mr. Mathews as he pulled
something out. "You made me jump through
hoops to marry your daughter and I didn't
mind because she was inexperienced, so
you had to protect her." Mike handed Mr.
Mathews the contents of the package. He
jumped up, "I can't..."

"What you can't believe your daughter is a
lying whore or that your daughter is
sleeping with my best friends boyfriend?"
Mrs. Mathews smiled proudly. Steven
turned around to Sydney. "I swear it was
before I knew she was with Mike and I told
you already." Toni looked at Steven. "I just
hired the PI a little over a month ago, so if
he sent those you're still sleeping with
her." Sydney walked to the front of the
church and snatched the pictures out of Mr.
Mathews's hand. "Toni didn't tell you
Syd?" Toni yelled from her seat. "What

picture because I have no idea of what you're talking about." Mike looked at Sydney. "They are pictures of Kelli with my boss and Steven." Sydney grabbed Mike's hand and whispered. "Mike this is not the place." Mike snatched his hand away from Sydney. "How can you defend this tramp, look her own daddy can't even look at her. Syd I love you, so forgive me for hurting you like Steven who deceived you. Syd we can put it all behind us. Syd, will you marry me?" Kelli ran in between them begging Mike. "Mike I can explain." Mike looked at her in disgust. "Explain what, that you have been lying to me all this time."

"The pictures are fake, Sydney wanted you for herself and she made them to break us up because Steven wants me instead of her." Mike turned up his nose as if he smelled a foul odor. "Get out of my face Kelli, it's over." Mike walked towards the exit of the church amongst the whispers and scornful stares. Steven met Mike at the door. "I'm sorry for not telling you, but I didn't want to hurt you like she hurt me by cheating on me with you." Mike wanted to punch Steven but Kelli ran up "Steven you know you want me back so you cooked up this mess with Sydney to break us up." Mike turned around. "Syd is that true?" Sydney looked around. Let's take this conversation outside.

Chapter 11

Sydney walked Mike to the side of the church and calmed him down. "Mike I knew Kelli cheated on Steven with you because he wouldn't marry her and I didn't tell you because you loved her."

"So you knew and didn't tell me."

"Yes but I didn't find out until a few weeks ago and you wouldn't believe anything I said."

"So you're okay with him cheating on you with her?"

"He didn't cheat on me because I knew he slept with her before we decided to become serious." Mike was in shock. "Mike she's the only one that cheated because she had been dating Steven for two years before she met you."

"Did he tell you when he met her at our house that night?"

"No."

"Then why are you dealing with him?"

"Mike he was shocked and since we were not serious I wouldn't let him tell me about it. Did Kelli tell you?"

"No, why would she?"

"Mike why are you still defending her?"

"I love her."

"Well marry her?" Luke walked up shaking his head. "The heel he should. That chick is dead to us."

"Luke I need to talk to her."

"Why, you saw the pictures."

"They could be fake."

"Fake if they were fake who sent them?"

"I don't know, maybe it was Syd and Steven."

"He still loves her Luke."

"I'm with Tina in this situation because love ain't got a damn thang to do with this mess."

"Mike, Luke is right."

"I love her and I think she loves me."

"She doesn't love you."

"Steven, shut up because you're the one that cause of this mess." Sydney jumped between Mike and Steven. "What did he do?"

"He lied about his feelings for her, so after he saw us together, he wanted her back."

Luke put his hand on Mike's shoulder.
"Mike I know you don't believe that bull
you're saying right now." Toni pleaded
with Mike, "You have us so walk away
from her."
"If I had you and you didn't know who put
the pictures on my doorstep?"
"I did." Kelli's mother walked in to the
middle of the group. "Mike you are a nice
young man and you deserve a good woman,
not my trifling daughter." Everyone stood
there in shock. "Mama how could you, I'm
telling daddy and he's going to cut you off."
"My husband is where he is because of me,
so that doesn't concern me. Back then they
wouldn't take a woman seriously, so I used
his name to market myself." Toni got
excited. "That's I had all of you followed to
protect my assets, but because I have a
daughter that's sexually irresponsible I had
to stop the wedding."
"But why did you wait so long?"
"I didn't realize how stupid Mike was. Baby
these are your friends and they had your
back but my daughter used you, so you
should have listened to them."

"I knew it." Luke yelled.

"Sydney, Steven hasn't been with my daughter for months, but she tried to break into his house several times and succeeded once."

"I told you Syd." Sydney smiled at Steven.

"So everyone knew she was cheating on me but none told me."

"We did, but Mike you said you needed proof because we were jealous."

"I think you should leave because I am about to announce your decision unless you're going to marry my daughter?"

Everyone looked at Mike. "The wedding is postponed."

"Let's meet back at our house, so we can resolve this thing." Mike, Doug and Luke rode together. Steven rode back with the ladies in Sydney's car.

When the ladies walked in Mike was pacing and mumbling. "Mike calm down."

"No because you guys knew and never told me."

"Mike Doug and I just found out today."

"Staci, Doug had to know something

because he was nasty to her at your dinner party."

"I was nasty because I didn't like her or the way she spoke to Syd." Toni walked over to Mike. "We told you, but you said we needed proof." "Syd had proof, but she hid the truth."

"I told you, but you said I was lying because I wasn't as good as Kelli, so I was jealous."

"Baby you don't have to explain yourself to him."

"What is he doing here, he's the reason our friendship is torn apart."

"You need to calm down and accept your responsibility in this mess and stop blaming everyone else. You blew off your friends for a cheap trick."

"Who are you calling cheap; Kelli was a classy woman that helped me reach my goals." Luke stood up. "I can't believe you're still defending that gold-digger."

"I'm done if you want Kelli back that's on you but I'm not doing this with you again." Steven and Sydney walked upstairs. "I'm with Syd Mike, so don't call on me or

Staci."

"Well you know where I stand." Toni picked up Luke's keys and walked out. Ten minutes later Steven and Sydney walked through the living room with her luggage.

Mike and Luke were the only two left. "I really messed up this time."

"Mike we all make mistakes, but we continue to live and learn."

"I guess."

"Look at me and Toni after all these years, but I fought Christine about getting married every day."

"After all those years of living together why didn't you marry her?"

"She wasn't the one." M

"After all these years you still love Toni."

"Mike life is a journey we take to find true love, so once I got over the pain I wanted her back."

"I guess I let my true love slip away because of fear."

"Our journey is filled with uncertainty, heartache, and setbacks, but it's up to the individual to determine what true love is worth. That means are you going to let those things stop you from embracing that love or reinforce it."

"After all these years I've finally lost my best friend."

"Syd will never give up on you."

"Man Syd is gone."

"Mike I'm going to tell you a little secret."

"What now Luke."

"Syd was saving herself for you since that night in college, but you were on a mission to find love everywhere else but where true love resided."

"My grandmother has always said the grass looks greener on the other side, but if you put in work on your own grass it looks and feels even better." Mike took a deep breath. "I guess I worked so hard on the other side, I let my grass die."

"Are we talking about women or grass because I'm lost now." Both men laughed at their mistakes and focused on their revelation.

Toni called Sydney. "Hey Toni."

"I just have one question."

"What is it?"

"Can you believe Kelli's mother sold her out?" The ladies laughed. "I was a little shocked, but I'm glad she did."

"I'll call you tomorrow because this day has worn me out."

"I know." Sydney and Steven drove to his beach house for the week.

Staci was walking around the house mumbling about her friends. Doug wanted answers, but didn't know how to approach her after the events that happened. "Doug, did you hear me?"

"No what did you say?"

"I think Mike should marry her anyway, what do you think?"

"Staci, who got you pregnant in college or were you pregnant?"

"What? Where..."

"Just answer the question."

"Doug, you know I..."

"You were not a virgin, so who got you pregnant?"

"You did."

"According to this paper that would've

been impossible." Staci started crying and told Doug about Cornell.

If Your Wife Is So Good...Why Are You In
The Bed With Me?

Follows a woman refusing to accept or
acknowledge the pain she's carried from
childhood. She seeks out unavailable men
for brief flings to protect her heart. The
only issue is that the men are good so her
flings linger. Alisha finally meets the man
of her dreams. She falls in love which
causes confusion in her strangely
comfortable lifestyle. Alisha chronicles her
exploits with an array of unavailable men
as she searches for the one who will make
her heart leap. Throughout her journey
Alisha struggles with her physical desires
for men versus her faith and morals.

Really was created to assist women in examining their actions and reactions, while reflecting on their heart condition. We all struggle with facing the truth about ourselves and taking constructive criticism is a struggle, but growing takes pruning. So prune yourself with this short self-reflection question and answer booklet.

- Have you been broken?
- Do you fear success?
- Do you love yourself?
- Have you settled for the wrong mate?